RAPPER SLOUGH * LOOKOUT SLOUGH * DEADMAN
LOUGH * SEVEN MILE SLOUGH * SAL
FISHERMANS CUT * SNODGRASS SLOUGH * HAY
RESS REACH * HOG CUT * CHAMPION SLOUGH *
OMATO SLOUGH * POTATO SLOUGH * HORSESHOE
END * SPOONBILL CREEK * FRENCH CAMP SLOUGH
NEW YORK SLOUGH * MAYBERRY CUT * SHEEP
LOUGH * DUCK SLOUGH * MALLARD SLOUGH *
ONKER CUT * MUD SLOUGH * THREE MILE SLOUGH
TWENTYONEMILE CUT * FOURTEEN MILE SLOUGH
MINER SLOUGH * PROSPECT SLOUGH * HOLLAND
UT * DUTCH SLOUGH * INDIAN SLOUGH * ITALIAN
LOUGH * MAMOU SLOUGH * MONTEZUMA SLOUGH *
ICTORIA CANAL * BABEL SLOUGH * TELEPHONE
UT * BARKER SLOUGH * WHISKEY SLOUGH * HILL
LOUGH * RIDGE CUT SLOUGH * MIDDLE SLOUGH *
ORTHER SLOUGH * WEST CUT * DISSAPOINTMENT
LOUGH * LOST SLOUGH * STEAMBOAT SLOUGH *
EAVER SLOUGH * ELK SLOUGH * HUNTER CUT *
IBERTY CUT * COLUMBIA CUT * CONNECTION
LOUGH * CUTOFF SLOUGH * EMPIRE CUT * RACK

STURGEON TALES

STURGEON TALES

Stories of the Delta

CHARLIE SODERQUIST

Watercolors and Drawings by Marty Stanley

BLUE BEAR BOOKS

Sacramento, California

Blue Bear Books
3121 Garden Highway
Sacramento, California 95833

First Edition

Printed in Hong Kong through PrintNet

ISBN 0-9661347-0-2

ACKNOWLEDGEMENTS

For her patience, support and tolerance, I dedicate this book to my wife Janie. I suspect that at some point in the creation of these writings she was certain that an affair with a mysterious Miss Sally was at hand.

For her pedagogy, inspiration and absolutely essential editing, I thank Carolyn Crane Love of Nevada City. I would have written nothing, ever, without her help.

Finally, for their steadfast faith and continued good humor, I give love and thanks to my two wonderful children, Chris and Jessica.

CONTENTS

I N T R O D U C T I O N

) began writing about water about four years ago. Because the Sacramento River flows behind (and sometimes through) my home on the Garden Highway, it soon became the touchstone of my water writings. But to understand The River beyond the snapshot passing through my backyard, I needed to explore it further: origin, terminus, The Delta between. That's a lot of water. Luckily, help soon arrived in two forms: one piscine, another human.

When Sally Sturgeon came aboard, discovering and explaining the geography, history and culture of The River was suddenly a pleasure, not a task. I was rarely bored; there were many days when the pre-dawn excitement of what she *might do next* would jolt me awake and lure me to the computer. And off she'd go on a new adventure. What a pleasure to know her.

Marty Stanley (he's the human) arrived as a collaborator just when I needed an excuse to complete and compile this watery series. Not only did he suggest (over steaks, peanut butter, and Bogle Merlot at Al the Wops) that we combine our two ways of looking at The River into one, but he served henceforth as my most loyal mentor and supporter. (It's not easy moving from science and business toward art!)

I am responsible for any factual inaccuracies (where fact was intended). Resemblance's of story characters to actual people is probably intentional, and should be taken in good spirit. Speaking of characters and intentions, the savvy reader will notice the shift of narrator between stories. It is intentional. Who is telling these *Sturgeon Tales* is important.

The genre here is, I suppose, best termed *creative non-fiction*. The reader is therefore warned: these writings attempt a mixture of absolute, verified, immutable **fact** (as best I can determine it) with sassy, silly, evocative **fantasy** (as best I can imagine it). Sometimes the distinction is fuzzy. Sometimes it even surprises me. When that happens, I smile.

THE FISH POND

There is a small fish pond in my back yard. It was built by me digging a hole in the ground between the kitchen window and a big tree. It is lined with polybutylene so the water does not leak out, and it is bordered by bricks and redwood. Its shape is a modified trapezoid; one side—the one nearest the tree—curved. It has a brick waterfall on the east end fashioned into an existing brick structure which is the outside of a fireplace inside my house. The waterfall is hooked to a pump sunk in the west end. The water molecules who live in the fish pond spend their time circulating from the west bottom to the east top of themselves, babbling down the two foot drop of the waterfall, splashing on their cousins and friends. I think that is their favorite part: that cascade ride down the protruding bricks attached to the fireplace exterior. *Look out! Here we come!* they say to the others at the east end surface.

According to the cardboard box that the water pump came in, the collection of molecules called "pond" take this ride about once each hour. The pump manufacturer knows this because she knows how many gallons per minute her pump pumps, given certain assump tions about the height of the waterfall, the gallons locked into my modified trapezoid, &c. I personally don't know if each molecule gets to ride up through the pipe and down the bricks once an hour, although I can follow the logic of the gal who built the pump and placed it in the nice box for me to purchase.

The fish pond does contain fish, although not always. Once, I drained the fish pond with gravity and a garden hose. It was the intent of the garden hose to only siphon most of the water out, leaving the little goldfish behind. Those goldfish were six-for-a-dollar-at-the-pet-store little. But a mistake was made, and two of the little goldfish went on a nightmare ride through the hose onto my back lawn. I got there just in a nick of time and put them back in the almost drained pond with the others. That ride—I said it was a nightmare, but I could be wrong; it may have been fun—is different than the once-per-hour-on-average ride of the water molecules who live in the pond alongside the little goldfish. For the fish, it was a once in a life time event. The water does the waterfall ride all the time. In fact, day and night, for the pump lady suggested on the cardboard box that I keep it plugged in always.

The electricity that makes the gal's pump run is a different story still. The electrons come from far away and then disappear. They don't go into the pond to live with the goldfish and the water molecules. They just go away somewhere. I don't know where it is that they go. If I called the Pacific Gas and Electric Company, they might know, as they generally know from where they came—like maybe the nuclear plant at San Onoffere or the oil burning plant at Moss Beach.

Or one of the hydroelectric plants in the nearby Sierra Nevada mountains where PG&E water molecules cascade from the top of very big dams and spin gigantic turbines hooked to tremendous generators of electrons who then walk down copper wires atop tall wooden poles and jump into the lady's pump so that my water molecules can take a fun ride down the brick waterfall. *Look out! Here we come!* they say.

MOUNTAIN MOVING WATERS

"And Noah he often saiD to his wife
when he sat down to d i N e,
I don't c A r e where the watEr goes
if it doesn't get into the W I n e."

G. K. Chesterton, *Flying Inn*, 1914

It's two days before Halloween, smack-dab in the middle of fall. I'm up here on a hill above Truckee, California, almost at the crest of the Sierra Nevada mountains, 100 miles east and 7000 feet above my home on the Sacramento River, surrounded by the activity of anticipation of the arrival of the change of season. The groves of aspen are variously between full-yellow and leafless, seemingly irrespective of place-measures like altitude, or sites disposed to mostly sun or mostly shadow, or wet bogs versus dusty hillsides. The native grasses, donkey ears, and lupines all beat their retreat toward dormancy months ago, not long after the Sierra Nevada began its monotony of blue sky, no rain, cool evening summer. Blue. Dry. Cool.

Less obvious are changes in the great pines and firs which have subtly dropped cones now hoarded by squirrels and chipmunks nesting in the rafters of my cabin and elsewhere.

My most inanimate companion (the word speaks to lack of movement, not life) is the granite of scarped ridges, boulders both clustered and isolated, and cobbles and pebbles worn by ancient glaciers and last year's erosion. It too is preparing for winter: its mottled surface darkening through a spectrum of grays as discernible as the chlorophyll-green to reddish-gold to banana-yellow Technicolor blur of the surrounding aspen, manzanita, and deer brush.

Of the least inanimate things—the animals—it is more difficult to speak. Many have flown, or burrowed in for the winter. Those who remain disallow keen observation by their constant scurrying about; a frantic tending to the final details of the change of season. But of all the things which live here, the ones that are my most favorite are also the ones most conspicuous just now by their absence—the *moving waters*.

Moving waters are tricky critters. Up here they like to use combinations of time, space and form to fool the novitiate observer: night-ground-frost, day-sky-snow, dawn-leaf-dew are some favorites. Clever variations on the mundane of day-creek-ripple and night-pond-ice, don't you think?

Up here most waters arrive in winter, dropping by as snow, staying as ice. Other waters choose fall or spring, preferring to visit with old acquaintances and to make new friends as liquid droplets.

As to being a fall water: it is troublesome. If you fall here too soon, you may bounce off the summer bone-dry Sierra Nevada dust and evaporate immediately, having visited no one. Yet, if you tarry and dally about too long in the clouds high out over the Pacific Ocean, and don't grab a weather front moving east until Christmas (some years, even Thanksgiving is too late!), you will not be a fall water rain drop at all—you will be snow. That is the worst for the wanna-be fall waters: to lose their liquid identity, transmutate into a flake or a hail, lay amongst strangers sometimes as slush. A fall water's nightmare: being late.

Veteran waters time it just right. They watch carefully from the Pacific until the early arrivals, like cannon fodder, have moistened the dust, penetrated a few millimeters, perhaps even generated a rill or a rivulet in a feeder stream-bed. That done, the vets rev-up their cloud engines, shift the weather front into overdrive, race across the Pacific adding other moving water passengers from stations along the way, bump over the Coast Range, skim the great flatness of the Central Valley to build up speed and—wham-slam-splash, smack right into the face of the protruding Sierra Nevada. The goal, of course, is to meet with their friends, holding to that promise of "I'll see ya' next time around" made the trip prior. It takes some practice to be a successful fall water. Some moving waters never quite get it right.

The spring waters are a different breed. They profess superiority to the winter castes of snow, hail, and ice, abhorring the individuality-quashing ten-day blizzards ("How could you even get to know your neighbors in a storm of that magnitude?" they exclaim). Yet they ultimately join those winter waters through their own warm rain promotion of the mass-melt known as *spring thaw*, co-mingling with the solidified brethren as if betrothed. Spring waters are prevaricators. My fall waters and I tend to have little truck with these springs.

I'm compelled to mention that, just now, walking outside at daybreak with a perspiring mug of coffee in hand, I saw some waters clinging to the leaves. These waters deserve acknowledgment, as they are permanent denizens of the forest. They are dew waters.

They come and go not by the season, like the others, but by dawn and dusk. They are busy little waters, hiding by day as humidity, floating quietly near the ground by night, coalescing with their pals just at dawn, and then sitting together on a blade of grass, a twig, a discarded beer can, chatting and kibitzing until the sun shines and the air warms, and then, off they go again. Busy waters, these dews. Other waters allow that these dews originated—whether as fall water drizzles, winter water snows, or spring water downpours. Yet, the dews purposefully stay over through the summers for the inevitable cycle of spreading away from and then joining together with their like-kind. Why they chose to stay has not been explained. Perhaps these are hyperactive waters, bouncing and anxious, trapped in the daily rigmarole of evaporate-condense. . .evaporate-condense. . .evaporate-condense. . .evaporate-condense. . . evaporate-condense. . .

Maybe I'm biased to the fall waters because I am here now, just shy of Halloween, observing the changes of autumn. I think not. Most of the waters I know maintain that being a fall water is the most rewarding and the most fun.

Waters in general acknowledge that the falls have a pretty easy time of it in finding their friends. Say that a pal from the last century happens to drop from his cloud a week before you. No matter. He is probably only down an inch, no more that two, and you can easily catch him once you too arrive, percolating your way down through the porous Sierra Nevada soil. Contrast this with being a snow water in the dead of winter. You miss falling by even *one day* in a big storm and guess what? Your friends may be buried in a snow drift down two or three *feet*. How would you ever get down there to visit them, or they up to say "hi" to you? No way. Waters who <u>choose</u> to visit the Sierra Nevada in winter are said by others to be, on the whole, curmudgeons and recluses. "How else to explain it?" the other waters note.

The other fun thing about arriving in fall is that, if you're lucky, you get to ride down a rivulet. Sometimes into a rill. In a great year, there may be enough of you that the rivulet turned rill turns to a streamlet. Once I heard some fall waters claim that they rode a full-fledged brook a couple of hundred feet before the winter waters arrived. That must have been something!

Snowballs are a different matter. Think of what *those* poor waters have to suffer! You're lying there quiet as snow atop some pals, perhaps enjoying a nice sunny day. Suddenly: you are scooped by a mittened or gloved hand, squished and compressed into a semi-round ball—*ouch! ouch!*—and thrown through the air. You pray to fall harmlessly back atop some neighbors twenty feet away. Instead, you're splatted to smithereens on a passing delivery truck, a red brick chimney, the back of a parkaed human head. What a life.

Real ice is a different matter. I've witnessed many winter waters befall that fate, having landed as snowflakes on my cabin's steeply pitched, baked enamel green, corrugated metal roof. Sometimes the roof waters get lucky: gravity (a good friend, generally, to all the moving waters) may help them slide off as a conglomeration, plopping atop drifts of snow friends who arrived naturally nearby.

Othertimes—like when I arrive late on a Friday night and fire huge hunks of dead pine in the cast-iron stove—the bottom-of-the-pile, lying-on-the-roof snowflake waters are caused to melt. Trickle, trickle, down they trickle. Approaching the roof edge, the trickles hold their breath, grimacing in anticipation of: **icicle!** An icicle that grows, then melts, then grows longer, then melts, and then drips to the ground only to freeze again. And stays frozen, long after the piles of arrived-as-snow waters have turned into snow melts, and run off and away. The iced waters stay, imprisoned in a crystalline lattice of doom and delay.

Being roof-melted ice is worse than the snowball fate, all the waters agree. Ice is *not* a moving water. Ice is the brother of Granite, though a black sheep one. Granite, at least, accepts its position in Sierra Nevada life: foundation to all other living things here, nobly immobile to a fault. I pay homage to granite.

But most of all I applaud moving waters. Many of them pass through my back yard, back home, as a collection called The Sacramento River. Some of them have played frivolous games of eddy, whirlpool and miniature maelstrom with my sturgeon friends down in The Delta. But just now, up here, the moving waters are very absent. That they will soon begin to arrive—under various disguises and in clever masquerades—is evident. That some other moving waters continue so as The River, back at my home is obvious.

But if few are here and only some are down there, where are the rest? If in only a few months—in winter, before the spring melt—there will be many, many waters here and lots of waters down there, where are the others now hiding?

The path of Trout Creek winds from a series of springlets up the mountain behind me to the Truckee River below. I crossed Trout Creek in several spots yesterday. It was running maybe two inches deep, a few feet wide. Trout Creek is resting, ignorant to the fact that it is not—even in the spring melt-off—a creek at all, for a true creek is a saltwater estuary of a small river or stream emptying on a low coast. Yesterday it behaved like a brooklet or streamlet; in spring an upgrade to Trout Brook or Trout Stream might be justified. Perhaps Trout Redd, or Riffle, or Rill, or Rindle, or Rivulet or Runnel should apply. Maybe Trout Influent, Trout Tributary, or Trout Course. How about Trout Trickle. But *not* Trout Creek, thank you very much.

I believe that all the waters that come here—whether fall, winter or spring—know ahead of time that they will eventually brook southeastward amongst The Trout, then cascade further eastward along Truckee River, and then dead-end in Pyramid Lake over in west-central Nevada. I was once puzzled by this, for if these waters intend to come back, they must come from clouds born over the Pacific. And yet they have headed exactly in the wrong direction, knowing full well, I am sure, that Nevada the State is not contiguous to Pacific the Ocean.

Contrast that to being an East Coast water that drops near a real creek, where life is simple. A hop, a skip, and a jump down to the ocean, suck yourself back up into the atmosphere, hitch a ride on the next passing cloud, grab a quick nap, ride that cloud over the shore to the appropriate place, and bombs-away—you're back to visit your pals in nothing flat!

My moving water friends of the Sierra Nevada chose a more challenging life. My water's got gumption. My moving waters figured a way to beat this major geography problem of dead-ending in a ho-hum lake in the Nevada desert. My moving waters are tough characters, and clever ones to boot.

They had a few million years to solve the problem while the colliding land masses (plate techtonics and all that) began popping a huge hunk of flat granite vertical, making a range, the nascent Sierra Nevada. Moving waters hanging around at the time could cipher the inevitable: Trout Creek was going to end up on the *east* side of the range, having no choice but to run eastward further (even *wrong*-named brooks can't run uphill). From a slab of protruding granite at the future site of my cabin on what was then simply a modest hill, one could gaze east toward a solitary, pyramid-shaped mountain (now the island in Pyramid Lake). To the west was another, quite vulcanous and always snow-capped, called Mount Shasta. The headwaters of Trout Creek sat right smack between. "Ah-ha!" said one of the moving waters. "Pyramid to Shasta," deduced another. "Let's talk to Granite," concluded a third.

And they did, carving out a deal with Granite whereby he left a tunnel beneath the emerging Sierra Nevada between Pyramid Lake and Mount Shasta. Granite even tipped the conduit just a tad so that the moving waters could coast downhill from east to west (waters are notoriously poor upstream swimmers!). The watercourse ended at the base of Mount Shasta, where the city of Mt. Shasta is now located. In fact, if you go to the city of Mt. Shasta's City Park, there is a handsome wooden sign—installed by the city of Mt. Shasta's Chamber of Commerce—next to a large bubbling spring that reads: **Headwaters of the Sacramento River**. The fact that the signage is incorrect and that the spring in question is *not* the true headwaters of the Sacramento is irrelevant to those moving waters who choose to exit from it.

The ride from Pyramid under the Sierra over to Shasta is tedious. It's so dark, say my moving waters, that you sometimes bump an old pal without even recognizing him. And it takes a millennium. But once you bubble up outta that spring and rise in the boil of your compatriots to the sparkle of daylight, it's a heck of an exciting ride home. You get to rapid and eddy over and around the rocks and boulders of the brook called Upper Sacramento; lake a while with other still waters behind Shasta Dam, resting for the 500 foot vertical, turbine-spinning chute down to the Sacramento River proper; watercourse a hundred-plus miles of levee-banked, constant-current river, interrupted only by the inflowing tributaries of the Yuba, the Bear, the Feather and (just past my place) the American; meander with the San Joaquin in the sloughs and anabranches of The Delta; backwater—you can feel the tide now—at the Suisun Bay playground of the great white sturgeon; gut through Carquinez Strait; channel with massive tankers and expensive sailboats in San Francisco Bay, waving occasionally to fog and mist friends hanging above; and finally flood tide out through the Golden Gate to join the rollers and swells and currents of the mighty Pacific Ocean. Home, sweet home.

For me, back at my home at dusk when The River in my backyard is so placid that its surface is consumed with reflections of the stately cottonwoods on the opposite bank, when I quiet myself on The River's edge and think about the many lives of my mountain moving waters, I can see some of them wave as they float by, and I can feel others, alive and talking, deep inside me.

GHOST SHRIMPS

"... sturGeon remain WiLd animals and no proGress in their domeSticAtion has been achieved. . ."

Professor Serge Doroshov,
University of California at Davis, 1985

My old friend Sally Sturgeon swam by my house the other day. I happened to be down on the pontoon boat at the dock installing my birthday present. It was presented by Janie, with whom I share the house on The River on the outskirts of Sacramento. Sally rose up from the bottom and finned me over. But instead of bubbling about the damn silt level or the dam discharges or the disposition of the multifarious collection of local crustacea—as she often does—she leapt into a business proposition. "Carpenter," she starts out, "have you seen this little book by Frank Kaiser called *Sturgeon Fishing Guide*?"

"Are you kidding?" I replied. "Kaiser is a god around here. That pamphlet is the bible of the bay. The man is an *Acipenser* genius. I have an autographed copy complete with a little note that says: *If you caught a sturgeon today, return the one you catch tomorrow.* The city fathers of San Rafael should declare his Lochness Bait Shop an historical landmark."

"Did you see the picture on the inside back cover of the guy leaning against the 122-pounder he pulled out of San Pablo Bay?" asked Sally.

"Sure did. What a beaut', though I don't buy for a minute the caption's claim that the guy used a fly pole to catch it."

"Was my sister's stepson," said Sally.

"Which one?"

"The taller one. The dead one."

"Oh, that one," I said.

"You're a jerk, Carpenter. Here I am, only fifty years old, and I've got yet another dead relative. I'm sick of seeing all this slaughter first fin or hearing about it later through the kelp vine. For Poseidon's sake, I wish I could do something."

Sally had a point. There is a smell of sturgeon death all through the bays forenamed Honker, Suisun, Grizzly, San Pablo, Richardson, San Rafael. The sturgies just love to ride the tides there, especially when the water is stirred up chocolate brown. But for the young and the incautious, those bays are slaughter water. Sturgeon slaughter water. That's why Sally keeps to The River between Marty the Artist's place on Steamboat Slough and the mouth of the Feather. Wouldn't ever catch her wandering San Pablo Bay where the other jerk snagged her sister's kid. When she wants to get away—say for her week vacation in August or the Memorial Day weekend—she'll current-down past Rio Vista and cut through Three Mile Slough over to Frank's Tract. Visit some friends, relax over a tule-root beer. Most of the *sapiens* there are fishing for cats and bass, or just motoring around looking at the above-water scenery and not fishing at all. Sally says: forget the Bays of San Francisco, the Napa River estuary, the Suisun mud flats; they're nothing but a below-the-Delta death-wish. Says it's a sturgeon's worst nightmare.

She'd dipped below to gill some oxygen, and reappeared. "I've got some other fishy business before the lunch time feeding frenzy hits, so let's get to the point," she said. "Shrimp."

"Shrimps?" I responded.

"*Shrimp*," said Sally Sturgeon. "Your old pal Tony Wong can call 'em shrimps like his folks do, but unless I don't read the slant of your eyes right, you be a plain living-on-The River white boy, and you're going to call them without an 's, singular or plural, dam you."

I tried it out. "Shrimp."

"That's better. Now here's the idea. Kaiser's little book and most of the Delta sturgeon fishing guides recommend grass shrimp, ghost shrimp and mud shrimp as the baits of choice. Right?"

"Heard so," I said.

"Okay. Now a grass shrimp lives naturally amongst the eel grass and your mud shrimp mostly habitates the mucky silt bottoms. That's how they got their names. Are you with me so far?"

"Grass shrimp, mud shrimp."

"And I'd like to see my relatives live longer lives. I'd like the little sturgie kids aspire to be even bigger than the 468-pounder I hear you *sapiens* claim as the California record. Dam! that's nothing compared to the old days. I've heard there used to be thousand pound diamondbacks living at the mouth of the American when Captain Sutter landed on her bank and built the fort."

"Longer, bigger," I agreed.

"And I'd like to see all my pals have more fun. My grand-daddy—beached-and-by-golly, I loved that toothless old *Acipenser*—once told me this fish tail of him and his buddies racing up the Feather River. They'd fin and tale up her like spring cohos charging the fish ladder at Grand Coulee Dam. When it got so shallow that they could hardly breathe, they'd call a halt, declare a winner. And then—if there were Indians fishing for salmon in the moonlight along the banks—they'd count out loud, all together *'One, two, three. . . moon it'* and stick their butts out of the water, simultaneously, like an Ester Williams' synchronous swim team. Looked like a whole grove of sawyers magically rising *en masse* from the bottom. Scared the Indians nearly half to death. Made my grand-daddy and his pals laugh and laugh."

"We want more fun!" I shouted.

"And safe lives too. If a sturge gets the urge to make a run out to sea, it should have a fighting chance against the gauntlet of party boats anchored off Point San Pablo. If a family wants to take a day to dally about the waters off Alcatraz—maybe rise up off the bottom, let the kids take a gander at the tourists—I'd like them to feel safe. Hook-me-by-the-tail, there's nothing I'd rather do than host a Labor Day weekend family reunion under the wharf at Old Sacramento. But how do you think I'd feel if some invitees got caught at the Rio Vista bridge trying to get up here?"

"Safe fish, un-caught fish," I said.

"Whether a sturgeon, white or green, prefers the Sacramento, the Delta, or the great Mother Bay by The City—or any of the lesser bays, estuaries, coves, anabranches, tributaries, sloughs or backwaters in-between—I want 'em to live long and healthy. Every last one of them, in the whole friggin' fish tank, from that damn Shasta to the Gate of Gold."

"Big fish tank, lots a fish," I chanted.

"You know what Carpenter? Before your fat-headed bipedal sapien relatives nearly emptied The River with bypasses and weirs and pumps for the pursuit of agriculture; before your kind nearly *buried* the Sacramento in sand and clay and silt from your greedy hydraulic mining of the Feather watershed in pursuit of flakes of gold; before *you* committed the biggest piscine-holocaust of all time—that 500 foot high intrusion of concrete and steel you refer to as Shasta Dam—this used to be a nice place to live."

And with that Sally dipped below the surface, drenched me with a splash of her tail, and disappeared into the murky water. It was just as well, for my back was aching from leaning over the side of my pontoon boat listening to her business-proposition-turned-diatribe. It's not easy, holding one ear right on the surface of the river to hear her. For example, the wakes of passing water skiers tend to flood my eardrum and drown out her words. While God endowed the sturgeon with substantial mass, tasty roe, and a mouth like a Hoover Hall of Fame vacuum cleaner, she neglected to give them much of a voice.

I got up, stretched, poured a cup of coffee from my Thermos, and sat down with *The Guide*, pondering the enigmatic Kaiser: promoter of sport fishing, purveyor of fine bait, protector of the piscine. Eyes closed, I absorbed the flow of The River, feeling the twists of current and delicate whirls of spinning pools soothe my stiff joints, dreaming to its silence. Duck quaking awoke me. I watched the modest herd sparate—then coalesce again, sharing the events, *quack, quack, quack*, the cycle repeating.

I returned to installing my birthday present next to the compass mounted the year previous. Friends are often impressed when I can tell them in which direction The River is flowing as we cocktail-cruise on summer evenings. I think the compass is also a great safety feature, though the county sheriffs seem more impressed with stuff like life preservers and fire extinguishers—maybe I'll get some of that stuff next year.

This year I got the altimeter. Unlike the compass—which is powered by magic forces sent south from a big chunk of iron drifting somewhere near the North Pole—my birthday present required 12 volts of local electrons. Luckily, the volts were accessible from a miniature Sears Die Hard that came with the navigation light installed two birthdays back. The light lessens the odds of a premature ending to an otherwise pleasant night cruise due to unfair competition for nautical space by forty foot power boats doing twenty-five knots.

After an hour, I had gotten the three wires previously dangling from the altimeter correctly connected to the two terminal lugs protruding from the Die Hard (there are six possible combinations; I proudly got it right on my fifth try) and flipped the little toggle switch to OFF to activate the birthday present (well, maybe I should have tried more than five). It lit up and up surfaced Sally Sturgeon, 6.2 meters above mean sea level.

"Hey Sally," I yelled, still standing on the middle of the pontoon boat and therefore uncertain she could hear me. "According to my nifty 12-volt birthday present, it's 6.2 meters downhill to the ocean from here. What do you think about that?"

She said nothing. She appeared unimpressed. Maybe because she was born and raised below sea level (I checked my altimeter dial: it had no provision for negative readings). But when I got down on my hands and knees and leaned my left ear to the water, an apology floated up: "Sorry about blaming you for the behavior of your whole dam specie. When I think of my dear old grand daddy and all my dead cousins and nieces and friends, my little eyes get all salt-watery and a wave of nostalgia sweeps over me, and, well. . ."

"Hey, it's okay. It's okay. How was lunch?"

"Didn't feel like feeding. I drifted to the wing dam at Bryte Bend, finned into an eddy behind it, and sulked in the silt for an hour. I've been doing that a lot lately; could be piscine-o-pause. But I feel better now, and I heard from some channel cats on the way back that a good crawdad hatch has commenced down at Isleton. I'll go there for supper and make up for the lost lunch. Speaking of eating, I never finished telling you my plan about the shrimp. Want to hear how you can help us *Acipenser* be happier, live longer?"

I took the bait: "How can some shrimp and I help you out Sally?"

"Not any shrimp. Ghost shrimp. Kaiser's book recommends ghost shrimp above all the others as the sturgeon bait of choice."

"Is it true? Do you like the ghost the most?"

"I'd swim a league to munch on the little critters. They are yummy. My grand-daddy once told me a fish tail about this humongous hatch of ghosts in the marsh at the mouth of Prospect Slough. Do you know the place?"

My "Isn't that where The River turns into the Deep Water Ship Channel?" prompted another Sally lecture.

"Don't get me started again on your crimes against nature. Prospect used to be a pretty nice place until you *sapiens* carved that trench as a shortcut to the Port of Sacramento. I lost a brother there six years ago, whacked unconscious by the propeller of a big cargo ship. He drowned. Can you even *imagine* being a sturgeon and dying that way? Why, if I . . ."

"Can we *please* get back to the ghost shrimp plan?" I shouted, but she had sunk from sight—hopefully just to gill a fresh breath of oxygen and bubble away her anger. I guessed right, for when she resurfaced, we were back with grand daddy's fish tail.

"There was a big old sturgeon named Bentley who lived on the west side of Grand Island, where Sutter and Steamboat Sloughs divide. He was a whopper and he was mean, which is unusual for a sturge. Any living thing that tried to get past his place, well. . . he'd just gobble it up. An unwary striped bass. Innocent frogs, salamanders, water snakes. Whole schools of salmon running upriver to spawn. A muskrat paddling at dusk to its den in the bank. A snowy egret perched on a floating log. . . motionless, its back to the river. . . staring intently down for a minnow snack—bawham!, that big bubba would grab it by its long skinny legs and suck it up whole, feathers, web feet and all. Sea Cranes—crafty little birds that normally habitate the streams near Nevada City—didn't have a prayer. Grand-daddy said Bentley's mouth was so big he could vacuum a beaver clean out of its lodge. Big fish. Big, big fish, that Bentley was.

"Bentley hears a couple of sturgeon going past his place bragging about this ghost shrimp hatch up on Prospect Slough. Ghosts-a-plenty, they were saying. By the way, he never ever ate another sturgeon, no matter how hungry he was. None of us do; we aren't *cannibals* for Poseidon's sake. Whether from vanity or idle curiosity, Bentley heads to the mouth of Prospect to check it out. And, Holy carp, there are ghosts thick as flies on a beached whale. Now, you can't hardly see a fresh ghost shrimp—they're translucent, opaque unless they've been out of water a while. But old Bentley could smell 'em, yes he could, and he just finned and tailed the other sturgeon out of the way and proceeded to inhale ghosts like nobody's business. Fed all morning long, rested a bit, and commenced to feed some more. My grand-daddy was watching. Said he never saw a fish eat like that. The sun goes down and Bentley's still suckin' 'em in. My grand-daddy goes to sleep. Sun comes up and there's the behemoth sturgeon, still doing ghosts like there is no tide tomorrow. By the third day, the hatch is finally done and there ain't a shrimp in smell. Bentley gave out a belch that broke the surface like a bubble of swamp gas trapped in the Delta peat for a millennium, nodded proudly to the audience, and headed homeward back down Cache Slough.

"But he's so groggy from three days of non-stop ghost-gorging that he makes the first left turn—up Miner Slough—instead of the second left, which would have been Steamboat and a straight shot home. And Bentley is so bloated from three days of non-stop ghost-gorging that he's about eight feet wide at the belly. Back then, Miner Slough was not a major thorough-fare for sturgies of even modest size. Those over a couple hundred pounds never tried it, even in the spring floods with an incoming tide. But Bentley's paying no attention, tail-wagging his way upstream half-asleep, expecting his place at the tip of Grand Island to come into view just around the next bend. Well, he gets to where Miner Slough makes a sharp and narrow turn east, and burrlummpff, bump, brushaquashaquash—he runs aground, and not just on the bottom. He's wedged in on the sides too. Pretty soon the silt that naturally flows downstream starts to pile up a front of him. A couple of sinker cottonwood trunks drift into his face. Twigs and branches and debris collect. A big turtle, not anticipating the roadblock, tips over and

sinks, becoming wedged against the growing heap of things, dead and alive. A family of beaver quickly builds a lodge and adds two feet of cut willows atop the heap. Upstream, Miner Slough rises commensurably, dislodging more river detritus left previously high-and-dry by the last spring floods. By dusk, Bentley is buried six feet under. By dawn, he is a goner.

"Today, if you go to that bend on Miner Slough, you will see a little island. An island anchored by the remains of Bentley, former king of the Delta sturgeon."

"That's quite a fish tail," I say to Sally.

"Yep," says Sally back, "and *every word's true*. My grand-daddy said so. Took me longer to tell it than I thought, though. I'm out of air. Be back in a minute."

With an ear full of water, I again stood up, vowing to invent a better method of fish listening. I wondered if the author of the *Sturgeon Fishing Guide* listened to fish, and by what means.

I tried to recall how Flipper's human friends had managed to listen to her (him?) on the old TV show. Maybe they faked it, dubbing in the sounds back at the studio; who'd know? At the aquarium on Cannery Row in Monterey there is a loud speaker aside a big tank, the occupants going *arrh, arrh* while you watch them pretend to be happy through double glass windows. I always figured the loud speaker was attached to an amplifier wired to hydrophones submerged in the tank. But maybe the aquarium managers play a continuous-track tape of wild fish sounds captured live from Monterey Bay. Would the tourists care?

Maybe for my *next* birthday Janie will buy me a hydrophone gadget that I could install next to the compass/altimeter twins on the pontoon boat. Would I have enough volts left in the Die Hard to power all this technology?

How about two tin cans with a piece of string held taut between; could Sally hold it in her mouth and talk at the same time?

How about a big plastic funnel with a piece of garden hose duck-taped to the end? Float the funnel over Sally's head and hold the hose to my ear. Why, I could sit in a deck chair and be comfortable. Keep my ear from getting waterlogged! Drink coffee and have a smoke and listen to Sally all at the same time!

A splash of water collapsed my dream of better listening through technology. It was Sally, back from the deep. Not having the requisite funnel, hose, or duck tape at hand, I again dropped on my belly and put an ear to the water.

"I'm ready to tell you the plan," she said.

"I'm all ear," I answered.

"Let's review. First, according to Frank Kaiser's little book—not to mention the *absolutely true* recount of the big bubba Bentley saga—sturgeon love shrimp whether *au natural* or hooked to a line tied to a pole held by a fisherman sitting on a bench attached to a boat. Number two, of the shrimp candidates, the ghost is preferred to the mud or the grass. And fact three: ghost shrimp are invisible. You with me so far?"

"I'm hearing ya', loud and clear."

"Fact four: the *Glomar Explorer* is anchored in Suisun Bay, near the collection of relics of past wars which you *sapiens* call 'The Mothball Fleet.'"

"Those ships have been parked there since I was a kid. Everyone crossing the Benicia-Martinez bridge has see them. So what?"

"Never mind *what*, now. Let me finish. Number five, it is my fish-wish that my fellow specie lead longer and happier lives. No more sturgeon slaughtering at the poles of your specie. Are we in agreement?"

"It's a free river, Sally. You can wish what you want."

"Right. Well, here's what I wish," goes Sally Sturgeon.

And what a masterful treatise it was. Her knowledge of the behavioral profiles of *sapiens* and *Acipensers* alike was astounding. Sally had to go down five times to replenish oxygen and I was forced to down two beers to get through the details of The Plan. When she was done, I was absolutely convinced we could pull it off, barring one missing ingredient: the man to run it. To celebrate, I jumped in The River and we played two rounds of Marco-Polo (she won both; the closing of eyes gave advantage to her better senses). Sally left for a rendezvous with some friends at the mouth of the American and I walked back up to the house to find a funnel, a hose and a roll of duck tape. Sally always teases me about the spelling of "duct" tape. I always reply: "Hey Sally, this is a River Story, right?"

Marty the Artist lives down in the Delta on Grand Island in a little two story white house overlooking Steamboat Slough. Sally Sturgeon lives there too, but in it. They share views of the slough and of life, as neighbors will, though from different perspectives. Marty the Artist has a little studio on the Sacramento River side of the island in the town of Ryde, which is where Alex was found on the doorstep. Alex was born on the banks of a different river—the Little Missouri—in Marmarth, North Dakota, 35 miles east of Plevna, Montana.

To the best of my knowledge, there has never been a live *Acipenser* in North Dakota (the *Scaphirhynchus* shovelnose and pallid sturgeon relatives don't count). Not even on a visit. Not even lost, like Humphrey the Whale who wandered into San Francisco Bay and up the Delta a few years back. Marty the Artist—who lives on Grand Island and therefore should know such things—says Humphrey's northern-most progression was right about where old Bentley sunk, decades prior. Sally says she actually swam into Humphrey, near Isleton, on his sojourn. Best she could understand—there was the usual translation problem—he'd befriended some steelhead at a pub at the Farralon Islands (they rise just outside the Golden Gate) and agreed to follow the anadromous (they run from salt to fresh to breed) third-cousins back home. It being late at night—and what with the day's reverie, the toasts to Nemo, Queeg and Ahab, the bad crab jokes—Humphrey lost the steelhead in the labyrinth of Delta sloughs, anabranches and backwaters. Pulled over for a snooze at what turned out to be Rio Vista. When dawn broke the summer sky and he broke the water to look around, mayhem broke loose on shore. Citizens and tourists and school children soon lined the levee, pushing and shoving for a front row spot. Snapping photos, tossing rocks, yelling advice. Befuddled and hung-over, Hump hove-to in the wrong direction and wandered further up the Delta for nearly a week. The Fish & Game folks finally herded him back to the main channel and pointed him downriver. Everyone assumes he eventually made it back to the Big Water.

Sally confirmed that she'd never heard of a real sturgeon in North Dakota either.

Alex was a solid man, past forty, principled. A drinker. Out of the house smoker—of cigarettes, not marijuana; wrong era. Weighted by neglected weight lifting and too many frequent flyer upgraded, front of the cabin, first class airplane meals. Now retired. Corning, California.

Alex was experienced in the capture of various animals such as ducks, antelopes and grouse, for he had lived in North Dakota after all, and, other than drinking, there's not much else to do there. There is water in North Dakota, but it tends to be here-and-there water, scattered in ponds and pokelogans, so Alex had never fished much. When he quit his job and moved to "The Olive Capital of the World" last August, he felt right at home. Flat, brown dirt under. Cloudless, blue sky over. Hot, dry air between. Other than the olive green groves that stretched for miles around, Alex might have thought he was visiting Plevna.

Out on a pleasant Sunday morning drive perusing the flatness east of Corning, Alex—in a very un-Plevna-like experience—smacked right into the levee bank of The River. Retreating west, then south, he hit another dead end at Suisun Bay. Returning north, a too-soon right at Orland yielded Hamilton City and The River again. Thrown into a Humphrey-like daze, he cast the wrong way homeward—downriver. Hugging The River's bank, sometimes riding high on the levee, mostly driving down on the rich former-flood-plain bottom-land waist high in rice, sugar beets, alfalfa, tomatoes, occasional feeder corn, sometimes sorghum, there came the town of Princeton. Elevation 84, founded 1858, named at the suggestion of a Dr. Lull after his *alma mater*, Princeton's fame is for the two-car cable ferry (cost you two bits, one-way) or for The Duck Club—a watering hole of some notoriety—into which he sauntered for a Budweiser-backed Old Grand Dad to calm his River-frayed nerves. Alex asked the bar keep: "What do ya' all do here in Princeton?"

"Farm."

"I could see that, driving here. Nary a hectare unplanted, far as I could tell," said Alex, recalling the fields of green interrupted only by occasional dirt cross-roads, irrigation ditches, power lines. Different than the dry-land, wheat and oat farming of his former state.

"Feeder corn, processing tomatoes, sugar beets," continued the bar keep.

"What I meant was: what do ya' do when you're done farming, like in the winter?" continued Alex, fondly recalling the slaughter of various North Dakota critters on sub-zero mornings in leafless aldered ravines and on ice-topped ponds.

"Shoot ducks, chase sturgeon."

Alex immediately recognized the first verb-noun combination, and said so: "Used to get teal, eider and mergansers by the bushel in North Dakota. We'd shoot 'em till the cows came home, which they never did, in the winter; cows lived inside, in the winter. But what's a *sturgeon,* and why would you chase it?"

"A Fish. Sport."

The ratio of words sent and received not in his favor, Alex drained his shot, polished off the beer, and headed down the road. Should have gone up the road, but no matter. One minute he's up on the levee spying The River; another, down in the rice fields eyeing agronomic prosperity. Up on the levee, down in the tomato harvest. Up on the levee, down in the droop of sunflower fields unwatered, drying for harvest. By the time he hit elevation 61 at Colusa (which must hold the River, if not the World, record for most previous spellings: Coluses, Colussas, Corusies, Colouse, Colusi plus Salmon Bend, the original name given by founder Charles Semple in 1850) he had been teased by the water so many times that a killer thirst had set in, and he pulled up to The Sportsman Club for another Bud, this time backing a Bushmills. "Say, miss," starts Alex, sliding a five-spot across the bar and eyeing the *please don't slam the dice* sign, "What do you all do here besides grow?"

"Hunt ducks, sturgeon, and pheasant."

At least a new and familiar specie has appeared, thought Alex. "I understand that this sturgeon critter is a fish," Alex bragged. "Exactly how do you hunt them here-abouts?" he added, not having gained a clue back in Princeton.

"Off the bank, in a boat—don't matter."

At The Islander Bar in Grimes (elevation 45 feet), named for Cleaton Grimes who settled near the bar in 1850, the flying critters were the same, but catfish was added, doubling the waterborne opportunities. The local secrets for productive cat-killing were shared by a fellow drinker of Budweiser and Jack Daniels in John McPhee detail. The list of required accessories (beyond pole and line) was impressive: Coleman lantern(s); simple bells or fancy electronic alarms attached to pole tips, intended to notify the (resting) sportsman of the arrival of the prey; seating devices (chaise lounges, deck chairs, inner tubes, foldable camp stools, discarded VW Bus seats, stolen football stadium benches, cottonwood logs laying, air mattresses leaking, bean pillows from the '60s); mosquito repellent; portable radios tuned to night games of the Sacramento Kings or the San Francisco Giants (season dependent); mosquito repellent; ice chests of Hamm's and Heineken; Thermos's of coffee, brandy-spiked and plain; extra poles, extra reels, extra leaders; weights and sinkers of ounces one-quarter to ten; hooks and lures; bobbers and floats. The bait was anything of non-plant origin, currently or previously alive: livers of various (carnivorous) animals, nightcrawlers (translate: expensive worms), crawdad tails (from crawdads caught incidentally), shrimps and prawns (the size determines the designation), squid pieces (never the heads, though), frozen and fresh sardines (two schools of thought here), smelt, clams (sans shells), and old hot dogs—*as long as they looked like they were trying to come to life*. No thoughts on catching sturgeon were mentioned, the cat man saying only: "What the hell would you *do* with one?" Alex agreed.

At The Sports Center bait shop and cafe in Knight's Landing (established by William Knight, previously of Indiana in 1843, at elevation 48 feet, for to farm The Land and ferry The River), Alex switched to Corona and Cuervo in hopes that it might change his sturgeon information-fishing luck. It didn't help. He was forced to hear that sturgeon are bottom feeders. "Use a spinning lure and you're likely to get stuck with a nice salmon, a trophy steelhead, maybe a fat striped bass," was the way the bar-keep put it.

Alex bypassed Sacramento (elevation 25) and staggered into a joint in Freeport (16), so named in 1862 because you didn't have to pay the shipping levee assessed by the big neighbor upstream. "Don't forget to bring a sturdy gaff or a 22-rifle if you expect to land the thing."

Careening into Clarksburg (11), lucky that 1849 founder Judge Robert Christopher Clark was long dead and gone. "Need steel-wire leader, plenty of line—hundred pound test."

Excepting the paucity of steamboats, Courtland Sim's steamboat landing was not much changed since 1860, the elevation still 5 feet above sea level. "My uncle landed a three hundred pounder right off the bank here in Courtland last fall using some kind'a shrimps."

Locke. If only Alex had come a hundred years sooner. The famous Chinese town: Tong controlled gambling, whores, opium dens. Tamer after fifty years: speak-easies, beers snuck to twelve year olds, firecrackers. Now: only Al the Wops, though arguably the best drinking establishment in the Delta. And the only anything establishment awake in the two block string of decrepit, tilted two-story wooden buildings split by a one way alley so far below the levee that the bar might actually be below sea level. Al the Wops: whole troops of Boy Scouts pursuing Hydrocartography Merit Badges sent out at high noon in clement weather with binoculars, maps and geo-synchronous satellite positioning devices have missed it. Alex—coaxed downriver by mystic fish forces, a hundred fifty miles and twenty drinks away from the olive capital of the world, in pea-soup fog you could eat with a fork, at one fifteen at night, his crania clogged with sturgeon trivia, his body effervescing ethanol—walks right up to it and in, yelling: "It's Miller time; a round for the house!" Alex tried to have social intercourse with Al's stuffed ostrich. Alex tried to bribe the Wop's still-Chinese cook into stir-frying a mess of shrimps, a slab of sturgeon, a filet of cat. Alex tried hustling a Hell

Angel's chick into an alleyway quickie. Pulled onward by the fish force, Alex stooped on his way to the door to retrieve a dollar bill dislodged from the ceiling, thus ducking the fist swing of the Angel chick's old man, thus avoiding pre-Sally's-plan death, thus able then to. . . reach the town of Ryde (which would have looked—had Alex been able to perform that physiological function—like the town on the Isle of Wight for which it was named) and which contained but four buildings: the Ryde Hotel, M&M Auto Repair, Reclamation District 3 Headquarters, and a half-abandoned post office building half-occupied by Marty the Artist. At an elevation immaterial. For Alex had arrived at the end of his journey, mistaking Marty the Artist's storefront display of River and Delta watercolors for yet another beer bar bait shop. Marty said only two things to the babbling Alex (that Alex can even claim to remember) before deposited him in the back room: "Not just any shrimps: ghost shrimps." And, "I'll call Carpenter."

For a fifty year old *Acipenser transmontanus,* Sally is as pretty as they come. Six foot six, a slender hundred ten pounds. If Frank Kaiser ever published a sex fishing guide, Sally would be the centerfold. Forty and two diamond-shaped plates ("scutes") down her sides, a white-gray-dusk-tan scaled back, four cute tubular sensors ("barbels") dangling from her proud snout afront her bottom-set, toothless, heavy lipped, feeding orifice that siphons crustacea, mollusks and small fish from the mucky bottoms of rivers and bays—she is a white sturgeon queen. Unlike her green (*A. medirostris*) cousins, she does not need to run to the ocean to initiate breeding, nor find a fresh-water tributary to do the final deed. Sally first laid at twenty three—a year or two earlier than most—and she's done eggs again four times since. Two of her first daughters have already made Sally a grandmother. I like the looks of Sally and her brood a lot.

I liked the looks of Alex less. He'd been on the floor in the back room of Marty the Artist's studio, comatose, for nearly a day and a half before Marty the Artist remembered to call me. Marty and his wife Sherry had dragged Alex's body across Highway 16 and down the levee to the Ryde Hotel dock shortly before I arrived on my pontoon boat. Sally's ride was briefer: a quick swim around the top of Grand Island. Alex's present morphological and physiological conditions, though damaged, were unlike those of sturgeon who (from the outside) are indistinguishable as to sex and who (on the inside) are, when young, more similar to a frog than a standard fish.

Various fashions of revival were considered, discarded. "Let's try eggs," Marty the Artist finally suggested. Sally nodded affirmatively. I had no better idea. Marty ran back up the bank to call his buddy Kip Korth at Korth's Pirates Lair, who pulled a jar out of storage and drove it over. We rolled Alex on his back.

"Anyone I know?" asked Sally as Kip spooned the black caviar into still-sleeping Alex's mouth.

"Rio Vista Bridge, October 1995," said Kip. "Eighty pound white. Two lip scars, been hooked before."

Trying to distract Sally from fretting over another dead relative, I said: "Laying on his back with that fat white belly and that open mouth, darned if Alex doesn't just about look like a sturgeon." I added quickly: "Though an ugly one."

Marty the Artist began thumping Alex's chest between Kip's spoon feedings, forcing the prone sturgeon-look-a-like to gasp and involuntarily swallow the fish egg delicacy. Marty the Artist and Kip were sharing finger scoops of the last of the jar just as Alex came to.

"Arrghh," said Alex, sounding somewhat like a sick catfish I had once befriended.

"Arggrrhhrrgg (wher) blahhergrick (em) schloggnick (eye)," said Alex, spying, through quarter-slit lids, the medical alert team assembled on the dock.

"You are in heaven," I said, according to plan. "Neptune, the fish God, has brought you back to life with the magic elixir, the piscine palate pleaser—*le Caviar de los Sacramento*. Soon you will be performing great acts of kindness and restitution. You will be a hero to us all, but especially to the living things whose eggs have saved you, and which you will, in turn, save back."

"Errbligehddarrgblk (eggs)?" said Alex.

"Yes, yes, quite right," I continued. "You see Alex, this is not North Dakota. This is California, once believed to be an island governed by the mighty Calafia, queen of an amazonian tribe of females. You have traversed and trailed—town by town, bar by bar—our mighty river, The River. The aqueous movement once called the Buenaventura, once the Jesus Maria. The watercourse once thought to flow through the Rocky Mountains from the Great Salt Lake. The mystic channel to the Northwest Passage. You are now duty-bound to be the protector of these ancient and royal things: the island of Calafia, the Buenaventura, and the white sturgeon—the cousin of Hiawatha's *Mishe-Nahma*. The eaters of shrimps;

er, ah, eaters of shrimp. Many shrimp. Mud shrimp. Grass shrimp. And ghost shrimp. Especially ghost shrimp."

"Thrimps?" said Alex.

"Shrimp. Ghost shrimp. Say *ghost shrimp*," I pleaded.

"Simps. Ghast simps."

"Try harder. Say it: ghost shrimp," I begged, testing him. Would this *sapien* Alex give us a sign? Say the abracadabra words? Sally was up on her fins, looking over the edge of the dock in anticipation.

Marty the Artist's friend Kip stopped licking his roe-soaked fingers. He stuck two of them into Alex's mouth, nudging aside the last few dozen eggs that were blocking the man's larynx.

"GHOST SHRIMPS," heaved Alex, awake and free of roe impediments. "GHOST SHRIMPS, ghost shrimps, ghost *shrimps*!"

"You are the chosen one!" I pronounced, knowing that we now could proceed with the plan, double plural or not.

"Yes. Yes, yes, yes," interrupted Frank Kaiser before I could finish with the details over the phone. "I'll write a new edition tonight. How fast can you get a thousand copies composed and printed?"

"With the help of my good friend Chris and the resources of Blue Bear Books (*Specialty Publishers of California*, reads their letterhead), a week, tops," I said.

"I'll have the text to the BBB Internet web site by morning," said Frank.

"Technology is cool," I said back.

The *Glomar Explorer*'s career was brief but stellar. She was secretly built (by none other than Howard Hughes) at a cost of dozens of millions for a one-time voyage, with a singular purpose: the retrieval of a sunken Russian nuclear sub. She succeeded. All this became public when it didn't matter anymore, in the '80s. I'd seen her parked with the Suisun Bay mothball fleet, but this was the first time I'd been aboard. I'd made an inquiry to buy her.

The guy from the General Services Administration apologized for the rusted-tight machinery (like the engine); for the flotilla of bilge pumps pumping 24 hours a day in perfect harmony with the inflow of Suisun Bay through a thousand cracks and rusted-out rivet holes; and for the abundance of rust in general. He kicked at it as we climbed ladders and ducked bulkheads. I finally asked him to stop, afraid he would kick a hole right through and ruin any chance of success at Sally's plan. It's hard to tell—having never before bought a four hundred foot hunk of leaky steel—but I think we got a pretty good deal.

We hung a flag from the tallest mast. It was designed by Marty the Artist and sewn by his Betsy-Ross wife Sherry while little Skyler Winslow Stanley napped. A smiling white fish on a crimson background. It flapped nicely in the Delta breeze.

Captain Mike of the *Star Mourning* was all ear when I called him in Crockett—a step ladder town of old stucco homes on the hillside in the western shadow of the double span steel bridge over the Carquinez Strait, the old C&H Sugar mill to the east balancing the scenery nicely—and inquired as to a sturgeon outing on San Pablo Bay.

"Fifty bucks a head. Another five for a one-day license if you need it. The *Star* can take twenty fishermen; fifty-five footer, toilet, radar. I supply all the equipment—rods, reels, line, sinkers, hooks, a net and a gaff—and a mate and the bait. You bring your own lunch and beer," said Captain Mike.

"I'd like to charter the whole boat. But there will be just three of us."

"Have to charge you for fifteen people, that's my minimum. That'd be seven-fifty," said Captain Mike with no pause for calculation. This issue had come up before.

"Mike, we'll be bringing our own bait. In fact, our bait will be already set to number two snelled hooks, steel wire leaders. Save you some money on hooks, line and bait. How about five hundred."

"Six-fifty is as low as I can go," said Captain Mike, fish guide turned capitalist pig.

"Six," I said, trying to keep The Plan within budget.

"Be on the dock behind the Nantuckett restaurant at seven, sharp."

GHOST SHRIMPS—SO FRESH YOU CAN'T SEE 'EM was painted in bold, ten foot tall white letters on the *Glomar,* port and starboard. Close enough, I thought, eyeing the double-plural Sally had broken me of.

"Nice signage Alex," I said as we approached the ghost factory in our skiff, flying a small version of the smiling white fish on red from the stern.

"That's nothing. Wait until you see the tanks and filters and pumps and other cool stuff down inside. It's a fac-tor-ee. I figure we can hatch and fatten maybe a hundred thousand ghosts a week. It's a ghost-o-matic."

Once aboard, I got the VIP tour. True to his word, Alex had retrofitted nearly the whole inside with a hatchery that would have brought saltwater tears to Sally Sturgeons' eyes if she could have seen it, which, of course, she couldn't. Sturgeon can't see worth a dam. Don't need to. Sturgeon smell when they want to find something. Sally probably could smell the *Glomar* from her home on Steamboat Slough, twenty two miles upriver.

Frank Kaiser's new book—*The Virgin Sturgeon, How To Get One*—was an immediate success. We brought an armful aboard the *Star Mourning* for Captain Mike to distribute later on his usual twenty fishermen a day jaunts into San Pablo Bay, where our party of three now commenced to sail. As promised, we also carried aboard a double-dozen sets of pre-hooked bait with steel wire leaders, prepared by Alex. We crossed the Pinole Shoal channel and anchored in five feet of water southeast of the Sonoma Creek estuary.

"Let's kill em'," shouted Captain Mike, jumping from his perch on the flying bridge to the deck where Chuck, the first and only mate, was staring at Alex's hooks. "What in hell's name is *this*?" said Mike, grabbing one and holding it eye level before me.

"An olive and three ghost shrimp," I replied.

"I see the olive," said Captain Mike. Chuck hadn't moved. Chuck looked befuddled. "What shrimps?" pushed Captain Mike.

"Three ghost shrimp. Here, let me count them for you," said Alex, moving into the conversation. "One, two, three," sliding his finger up the shank of the hook past the olive, which was visible to all aboard.

"Don't see no shrimps."

"Harvested just this morning and kept on ice on the ride over," said Alex. "So fresh you can't see 'em, just as advertised."

"Bull sheet."

"The olives are from Corning, up in the Sacramento Valley," said Alex, a flat and brown vision of his North Dakota past flashing through his mind. "Best olives in the state, maybe the world."

"Sheeet."

I joined the conversation, such as it was: "We've come here to fish Captain Mike. Let's get to it, if you don't mind."

Marty the Artist landed an eighty-six pounder on his first cast, portending the fish frenzy to follow. We hooked, netted, and released sixteen diamondbacks before lunch, each over the legal limit of six feet, each swimming away unharmed. Captain Mike was incredulous (first mate Chuck had long since disappeared below). I offered him a beer. Against Coast Guard regulations, he chugged it. I showed Captain Mike *The Virgin Sturgeon, How To Get One* book, hot off the press.

"Frank Kaiser wrote this? <u>The</u> Frank Kaiser?" doubted Captain Mike.

"Brand new edition," I said. "Complete with his latest thoughts on how to snag 'em, and big. Like today. Look, here's Kaiser himself holding one of our new olive and ghost shrimp rigs."

"Don't see no shrimps."

"Like I told you Captain," interjected Alex, "Like the sign on the side of our *Glomar* hatchery reads: 'So fresh you can't see 'em.'"

The afternoon went about the same. By the time we headed back to the dock at Crockett, we had a convert. Sally Sturgeon's sixteen friends—no worse for wear other than a few cut and bruised lips—had done well.

Word of the latest and greatest bait spread like the red tide on a Florida beach. The first run of Frank Kaiser's tome sold out in a week, making writers of fiction and fact from San Francisco to Davis flush like a Carquinez Strait rip tide with envy. For about three weeks, Captain Mike and his party boat competitors hooked over-limit whites and even greens (word had gotten out to the other specie, who made a deal with Sally to be included in The Plan). Hooked 'em like kids at a two-bits-a-fish trout farm. The sturgeon were always too big to keep legally and so were nearly always sent back, after the obligatory photo, the tabulations of length, the exaggeration of weight. Those who gave their lives were remembered by those who did not.

By week four, the party boats and self-propelled fishermen of Honker, Suisun, Grizzly, San Pablo, Richardson and San Rafael Bays noticed a slowing. But knowing that a fisherman's luck ebbs and rises like the tides of the bays they were attacking, the sturgeon hunters kept casting hooks of invisible ghost shrimps plus an olive, purchased from the *Glomar* entrepreneurs.

After a month and a week—well into the seventh printing of *The Virgin Sturgeon*—bay sharks with a newly acquired taste for Corning olives were outnumbering the sturgeon brought on board ten to one.

By week eight, not a single sturgeon—white or green—was being hooked in any watery placename ending with Bay. And the *Glomar Explorer* was conspicuously absent from the one first-named Suisun.

Frank Kaiser took over the retail side of the invisible ghost shrimps plus olive business. He still makes a heck of a living placing a four cent Corning California green on a twenty cent number two hook and selling the assembly for a buck ninety five. "The three ghost shrimp on there are *really expensive*," he explains to objecting bait buyers, who buy the thing nonetheless, plus a five dollar plus tax autographed copy of *The Virgin Sturgeon*, *How to Get One*. Frank now writes: *If you don't catch one today, go back out and try again tomorrow*, in contradiction to the inscription on my copy of his original—the *Sturgeon Fishing Guide*—which has become quite the collector's item.

The *Glomar*, though engineless, had sailed upstream one moonless, starless night. A night so foggy it was nearly airless. The physic of the borderline of water and air was so obscured that second year salmon passing through the Delta leapt high above the water's true top, lost vertically. No boat dared ply the waters except the fog-stealthed *Glomar*, which moved magically upriver against the current, a glimmer of the wakes of a thousand sturgeon tails trailing behind.

SO FRESH YOU CAN'T SEE 'EM has faded from the sides, up past Cache Slough, beyond the turnoff to Sally Sturgeon's place on Steamboat. Hidden in an unnamed backwater near where Bentley had ghost-gorged all those years back, the *Glomar* now farms real ghost shrimp, hundred thousand a week. Alex pumps in some water, pumps out the shrimp. Every other Wednesday he does a chef's special of mud shrimp just to break the monotony. Grass shrimp have become a Christmas Eve tradition.

Thanks to Sally, when the *Ancipenser transmontanous* get an urge to ride the tides in Carquinez Strait, or if relatives from upriver are in slough and they all want to go down to Alcatraz to gawk at the tourists, the sturgeon can now do so without fear. For, thanks to Alex, they now depart the Delta with their tummies full.

DUCK-FUCK SEASON IS IN HIGH GEAR

"WhO k n o w S who first sprayed
WD-40 braNd lubricanT on his bAit
and discovered that,
s o m e t i m e s , sTurgeon
will prefer the taSte?"

Larry Leonard, *Sturgeon Fishing*, 1992

My interest in living things is tilted toward the piscine, though moving waters too are alive and receive considerable amounts of my attention. Given that, visitors are surprised at the quantity and variety of above-water living things that I allow here in my backyard on the edge of the Sacramento River: ducks mostly local (a few always seem to be passing through); geese, though they bed for the night three doors up; egrets and heron fishing the banks for minnows; river otter (seen only once); beaver slapping tail at dusk. That last one really gets them. *Beaver in Sacramento?* they exclaim. The land and the trees, mostly cottonwood and willow, teem with the standard country critters: squirrels, magpies, crows, opossum, fox, pheasant, raccoon; this surprises only the most city-bound. I'm not a naturalist— I don't know the legal names of any of these non-piscine living things. White sturgeon are *Acipenser transmontanus*, which is plenty enough backyard Latin for me.

In sheer quantity, the ducks dominate. There's a weird black type, heads marked red and white. We call them chicken-ducks because we've never seen them fuck like all the other ducks are doing this week, and therefore suppose that they breed across the levee road with the barnyard animals for which they were named. The other ducks look like ducks should, and they are currently fucking like crazy, it being the season.

It got so bad this morning that the backyard ducks were actually flying in the air and sitting high in the trees. That may sound funny to you since ducks are, after all, birds (aren't they?) and birds are supposed to fly. Well, it's an unusual sight here in the backyard; I'd concluded that Mother Nature had permanently grounded the backyard duck air force, whatever her reason. But it was not the case this morning: the girls were flying away from the boys, and the boys were flying after the girls like an air show reunion of barnstorming biplanes. You'd see two ducks flying around, then they'd stop to catch their respective escaping and chasing breaths by sitting in the trees, then they'd start flying around again. I don't think they can fuck perched in the trees. I've never seen a pair fuck in mid-air. All this flying around will eventually end when they return to the top of the water, where they belong, and the actual fucking commences, as it should.

In a month or so all this ruckus will have ceased. The ducks will float and paddle on the interface of water and air with ducklings in tow. There usually are two, three families in the backyard, each starting with a dozen members. Attrition sets in, as it should, and only one or two of each of the new quacker families survives. The backyard always has a steady-state of grown-up ducks after the completion of the duck-fuck cycle. I don't know if this results from the new ones flying away and the old ones dying, or the old ones flying away and the new ones dying, or some other combination of flying-dying that leaves just as many as we had at the start of duck-fuck season. Like I said, I'm a piscine kind of guy.

It occurred to me that I may have misinterpreted all the duck flying and tree sitting that transpired earlier this morning. Maybe there was something lurking in my backyard just below the surface of the muddy brown river—waiting patiently for a nice fat boy duck or girl duck distracted by the potential of procreation—that kept them airborne. Come to think of it, I've seen baby ducks sitting on top of the water just disappear—poof!—a ringlet of tiny wakes circling the locus of death. Maybe that's how the balance of backyard ducks is maintained. Something piscine doing duck-sucking in perfect harmony with adult quackers doing duck-fucking. I asked my friend Sally Sturgeon about this when she finned by the dock for her usual Sunday morning visit.

Sally said it was a well known fish-fact that the cats in my neck of The River eat ducklings. Especially the really young, juicy, tender ones. Sally said the cats roll on their backs, slide right under the unsuspecting youngsters, and just sort of inhale 'em. I asked her why sturgeon (who have a vacuum mouth on their bottom that would qualify for the Hoover Hall of Fame) don't participate in this baby duck genocide. Sally said her kind don't care for the little web feet; gives most sturgies a tummy ache. I reminded Sally that she and her relatives eat a lot of clams, whole. She reminded me that sturgeon have a gizzard, so the clam containers aren't a problem. But the rubbery little feet don't grind up worth a dam, she said.

"My grand-daddy used to tell me about a big old mean channel catfish who lived way down-river from you, past my place on Steamboat Slough. This cat's name was Mumford. Didn't have a single piscine pal in all the Delta waters, he was so grumpy and mean. Mumford was a duck sucker *par excellence*. Hung out mostly at the mouth of Tomato Slough where it flows into Seven Mile Slough."

"Past Isleton?" I asked.

"Even farther down The River, past Rio Vista. Take the exit at Three Mile Slough; Seven Mile will be your first slough on the left," said Sally.

"Got it," I said.

"Grand-daddy said that this old cat Mumford was as big as me. Of course, he told me this story when I was only twenty years old. So Mumford must've been smaller than the six-six, hundred-ten I am now. But that's still dam big for a catfish. Dam big, don't you think?"

"Damn biggest catfish I've ever heard a tail about," I said.

"Hey. Grand-daddy didn't tell no fish *tails*. He told fish stories, and every one of 'em was true. He said so. There's a difference between a story and a tail!"

"Okay, okay. Go ahead with the *story*," I apologized.

"Accepted," said the sturgeon queen. "So Grand-daddy was coming up from San Pablo Bay—he always wintered there because of the abundance of ghost shrimps—to spend Christmas Eve with us in Steamboat. Instead of coming straight up The River, he decided to take the back way for a little change of scenery. Just east of Suisun Bay, he veered toward Big Break. Then he finned up Dutch Slough and across Sand Mound Slough over to Frank's Tract where he stopped to shoot the bull and have a few tule-beers with a couple of old cronies. Grand-daddy knew the detour would take most of the day, but he also knew we wouldn't dare start opening the presents without him—he being the patriarch and all—so he didn't rush."

"But it took even longer than he'd planned, what with the stories he had to embellish and lengthen just to stay even with the other old codgers hanging around Frank's. Finally, with a hearty toast of *Merry Christmas to all*, he got back on the waterway at dusk, heading north through Fisherman's Cut toward the Stockton Deep Water Channel."

"Did he get to Steamboat in time for Christmas Eve?" I asked Sally.

"Don't interrupt my grand-daddy's story. He's making good progress, in spite of a belly of beer, finning and tailing along with the rising tide, when he comes to the Three Mile Slough-Seven Mile Slough junction. He smells all this commotion up-slough to the right. If he turns left, it's less than a mile to The River and an easy swim to Steamboat. But my grand-daddy—he was a curious old *Ancipenser*, Neptune bless him!—well, he just can't stand not knowing what's happening up the other fork."

"Since you don't have a chimney in the slough where you live, how does Santa Sturgeon get presents to you?" I asked Sally.

"Why do you keep interrupting? *You're* the one who brought up the disappearing duckling dilemma. Do you want to hear about Mumford the monster duck killer or not?"

"OK, OK, you're right. Go ahead with your grandpa's fish tail. Err, oops, fish *story*. Sorry."

"So Grand-daddy surfaces and checks the moon for the time, figures he can still make the Christmas Eve festivities if he doesn't dally too long, and hangs a right instead of the left. He makes his way up Seven Mile Slough real slow and cautious like, one swing of his tail at a time. Pectoral by pectoral, knot by knot, he gets closer to the ruckus. He currents-up to a striped bass nestled in the tules and asks what's going on up ahead. Striper just smiles at him, won't say a word. Dorsal by dorsal, foot by foot, he creeps forward, along the edge of the bank. A family of muskrats are out of their nest, looking upstream. Asks the eldest what's all the commotion. Rat just smiles, won't say a word."

"Do you get to open any presents on Christmas Eve, or do you and your brothers and sisters have to wait for the morning, after Santa Sturgeon has come to visit?" I asked Sally.

She ignored me this time, and continued. "Inch by inch, fin to tail, tail behind fin, Grand-daddy moves on. He pokes his barbelled snout through the last of the tules and lo-and-behold, there is Mumford, splashing and thrashing like a sturge with the urge. By the way, Grand-daddy always liked that saying. It means. . . well, you know; what the ducks were trying in your backyard this morning. Anyway, there's that old, mean, duck-sucker cat, flopping flat on his back in the mud on the bank, trying like the devil to shake free. But he can't because he's swallowed the feet practically right down to his intestines. And they're big, wide webbed feet to boot, both of them. Can't spit them out. Old Mumford, he'd finally overdone it, got a little too greedy. Grand-daddy said it was the biggest blue heron he ever saw. What a commotion: the heron is flapping its wings trying to get airborne, Mumford is flopping around trying to un-swallow a pair of size twelve web feet, and critters from each and every anabranch, backwater and bayou for miles around are lined on the banks or float-ing in the water, cheering the heron on. Finally, with a giant surge of its wings, the big blue gets airborne, old Mumford in tow, hanging upside down."

"So then what happened?" I asked Sally.

"Well, Grand-daddy wished a Merry Christmas to all, and bid them all a good night, and surged up to Steamboat. All my brothers and sisters, even Pop and Mom, had given up and gone to bed, but I was there wide awake when Grand-daddy finally arrived. 'Grand-daddy,' I said, 'Guess what I saw while I was waiting for you?' 'What'd you see Sally?' 'Santa and his sleigh flying across the moon, heading this way.' And that's when he sat me down and first told me the story of old Mumford and the blue heron. That Christmas Eve, back when I was only twenty years old."

"So what did you get for Christmas that year?"

"A pair of green and blue plaid fin warmers," said Sally, and with a splash of her tail she was gone, heading back downriver to her home on Steamboat Slough.

I think Sally still has them. I remember her wearing them one cold Sunday morning a few duck-fucking seasons back. Personally, I don't care for green and blue on a gray-black fish like a sturgeon. But then, I'm a little fussy about things like that, being a piscine kind of guy.

S A L L Y   G E T S   L A I D

"WheN on the n a v i g a b l e   riVer
                i navigated like the SWAns,
        plaCing my barge in danGer,
        and m a d e   such H U G E   wavⒺs
                    with my huRRicane vErses,
        we a L l fell intO the wateR.

There the FiSH o b s e r v e d   me
            with cOld, reprOachFul eⓎeS
        while sarcAstic crayf i s h
                    thReatened our boTToms."

                            from *Precious Stone, The Yellow Heart,*
                            Pablo Neruda, 1974

Ｓally Sturgeon announced in mid-January that she was about to do it, could feel it coming. She's fiftyish, early fifties. How early we are not sure. I was born in a Palo Alto hospital on dry land in 1947. She was born somewhere in the Delta, maybe in '42 or '43. Her mom's been dead since the winter of 1985, hooked on a mud shrimp in San Francisco Bay near the Dumbarton Bridge. Her grand-daddy—his name is Ossian, though Sally just calls him "Grand-daddy"—has been dead longer. Sally and I figure he made ninety. He was a great teller of fish tales. She was a teenager and one day he was just gone. She doesn't know what happened.

   Sally Sturgeon first laid in her early twenties and has done it every eight years since, plus or minus. Keeping with sturgeon tradition, her children were named only after it was worth the bother. In Sally's family, they've always done the naming party at year two. Of the first brood, Arlene and Aretha are still alive. In fact, they made Sally a very proud double-grand-ma just a few years back. Arlie, Sally's first boy, hasn't been seen in years. Sally hears through the kelp vine that he's around The Bay somewhere, but he never comes up to Steamboat Slough where she lives. You know how thirty-something year olds are.

I've only known Sally going on a couple of years, so I was a little surprised to have been invited to the fifth laying. Arlene and Aretha passed; their lives were pretty hectic, what with the kid's school activities and the spring flood and all. Miss B declined immediately. She's a shy one (even by piscine standards) and, as the sole survivor of the second brood, she's rather special to Sally, so it was just as well. Next in line were the offspring with names beginning with C and D. Teenagers or less. Enough said.

You might say I was invited by default. I like to think there's more to my relationship with Sally. You can decide later.

The big surprise was where she decided to breed. White sturgeon are expected to do it in deep channels of quiet Delta sloughs. In the past, she'd stuck with protocol. But this time she opted to try it like her distant relatives, the green sturgeon, who go far upstream to the gravel beds of various Sacramento tributaries, like the Feather River. Which is the one Sally picked. As you might expect, the whole thing caused quite an uproar in the *Acipenser* social circles.

I've been asked why she broke with white sturgeon tradition. Tell the truth, I don't really know. Given her age and prior reproductive success (three As, a B, handful of Cs, and a pair of Ds ain't too bad a record!), you'd figure she'd leave well enough alone and get laid in the Delta. And given her local fame as the grand daughter of Ossian, you'd figure she'd coast on through to old age—maybe even hit a hundred if she was careful to check the crawdads, clams and shrimps for the hooks, lines and sinkers of fishermen before she inhaled them into her gizzard. You didn't know that sturgeon have a gizzard?

Some folks—*sapiens*—and piscine types alike—say it's all my fault. Say she did it to prove something to me. Prove she was different than the run-of-the-river *Acipenser transmontanus*. She's already different, I tell them. Sally can talk for Neptune's sake!

It's not that I haven't pressed the issue. I've asked her about this one-upping the greens thing a dozen times, both before and after we went up the Feather. She'd just curl up her barbels (those are the four "feelers" that dangle from the bottom side of her snout) and swing her head sideways. Like I said, truth be told, I just don't know. She's different, I can say that for sure.

We settled on a Tuesday in early April to head up the Sacramento. Winslow Stanley—Sally's young land-borne neighbor who lives aside Steamboat Slough in the white, two story, restored farmhouse with the lone palm tree, just up the road from the Grand Island Mansion—hosted an egging-away party the Sunday prior. Janie (she's my wife) and I attended along with Winslow's parents—Marty the Artist and Sherry. All the local river critters were also invited, and many came, at least for a while. A couple of old codger catfish made jokes about Sally; those standard "sturge got the urge" jokes. You've probably heard them all. Three uninvited white sturgeon from Rio Vista stirred up the silty slough bottom with comments about Sally's maverick ways. "Uppity bitch; too good to lay with us; Feather River indeed," and stuff like that.

But by and large, most of the other locals—the crawdads and striped bass and muskrats and beaver and herons—were supportive; they've known Sally for a long time. Everyone knows of old Ossian, her grand-daddy, and I think that helped get Sally some extra respect.

We *sapiens* sat on the bank with our feet in the slough, sipping on cold Red Stripe beers and snacking on roe given to us by one of Sally's sisters, rinsed and salted by Marty the Artist earlier in the day. Winslow (he was named after Sally's great grandfather) paddled around on his little foam swimming board, face down in the water, watching the aquatic half of the party. The other critters chatted and commiserated and snacked on each other. It's their way. All in all, it was a grand send-off.

When Tuesday morning came, I was packed up and ready to go by dawn, waiting out on the back deck, sipping coffee and watching The River wake up to the sunrise. Watching it close, for it was in spring flood and had decided to cover my whole back yard, right up to the edge of the patio. Sally surfaced about seven, and bubbled *let's do it*! loud enough that Janie heard the commotion from the kitchen. Janie ferried me out to the dock in the rubber raft and kissed me good-bye. Sally didn't bother saying good morning or good-bye directly to Janie; Janie doesn't hear sturgeon very well yet. I climbed aboard my pontoon boat and looked over the equipment and supplies: depth finder, altimeter, and extra gasoline; anchor, rope, and fishing pole (just kidding); grappling iron, binoculars, and captain's chair; sunscreen and salami; cheese and bread; candy bars; ice chest full of beer. Everything necessary for a River trip.

Sally finned over to the side of the pontoon boat and said: "Let's go, Carpenter. My belly's the size of a watermelon. Cast off, for Poseidon's sake."

"I'll meet you at the mouth of the Feather," I answered. "It'll take me about an hour and a half." Satisfied, she dove to the bottom and commenced upstream. The pontoon boat and I followed. About twenty minutes later, when the motor finally agreed.

I've boated from my place up to the merger of the Sacramento and the Feather many times; it's always a pleasant cruise. That Tuesday morning was no exception. I passed homes and docks clinging to the east levee; the Taylor Monument (a granite spire on the west bank erected in memory of Leonidas Taylor, captain of the *Steamer Belle,* sunk by a boiler explosion on the fifth of February, 1856); the Alamar marina under Interstate-5 (the bridge's underside is plastered with mud nests of swallows who zoom and soar and chase the boaters during spring hatchings); Zamora landing; Verona Joe's bar and grill.

The high water had generated many sawyers and planters. Islets of earth calved from the banks drifted past. The swollen top of The River was a mess. I dodged the floating *sapien* detritus—a volleyball, liter-sized soft drink bottles, a Styrofoam lid lost from a Styrofoam ice chest, aluminum cans formerly filled with Bud and Hamms, a plastic lawn chair left (no doubt) on the bank by a disappointed catfishermen, NO WAKE!-5 MPH ZONE!-buoys ripped from anchor, a 55-gallon steel drum. And I bumped over a good number of sinkers and sawyers, even though the pontoon boat draws less than a foot of water. Sally hugged the bottom as usual—twenty, thirty, sometimes forty feet under—oblivious to the junk passing overhead.

The Feather River, depth-wise, is another matter. There is a huge sand bar across its confluence with the Sacramento. I once ran into it doing 30 in a ski boat in the low (albeit not low enough to make the bar visible) water of summer. Some months later, trading beers for stories with an old river rat in the bar at Verona Joe's, I was informed that *everyone* knew the bar was there. I asked how. He wasn't sure about everybody *else,* but said *his* first hint was when he saw a guy standing in the middle of the river, knee deep, fishing. I offered that had one of Sally's relatives been cruising by, not paying attention, the fisherman would have been knocked right on his rear. He said that big white sturgies never came that far up The River anymore. I said that *everyone* of the sturgeon I knew went up there quite often.

At this, the old river rat slowly tipped his empty bottle upside down and stared straight at me. It wasn't until I signaled the barkeep for another round that the old guy gave me a wink and a nod of acceptance.

The sand bar wasn't there when the first *homo sapien* whites came exploring from Yerba Buena, naming the Sacramento and the Feather variously, and interchangeably, the Buenaventura and the Jesus Maria and the Rio de las Plumas. The names got settled in the late 1840's, two decades prior to the creation of the sand bar and the clogging of much of the Feather up to its confluence with the Yuba. Entire mountains were washed downstream through the Yuba as a result of the *sapien's* hydraulic-mining pursuit of gold. The Yuba was called the Yuboo by Captain John Augustus Sutter who arrived downstream to built his Fort in 1839 . Called the Henneet by Jedediah Strong Smith, the famous mountain man and explorer, who was the first white to see it, 14 March 1828. I've asked Sally what the white *Acipensers* called it before the white sapiens showed up and made a mess of the place. She doesn't know.

On account of the spring flood, the sand bar was now ten feet under, nearly "mark twain" (which is two fathoms which is twelve feet). I headed into the mouth of the Feather, cut the engine, tossed the anchor, and popped a beer. Sally broke the surface and splashed me with a flick of her tail. I got down on my belly, hung my head over the side, and put an ear to the water to hear her speak. (Unfortunately, I'd left my high-tech sturgeon listening device back home—it's a big plastic funnel attached to a piece of garden hose with duck tape so I can listen vertically, and avoid eardrums full of silty river water.)

"Where in Poseidon ya' been?" asked Sally Sturgeon.

"Been thinking. Thinking about previous jaunts up here," I replied. "Got here as fast as my 30-horse Yamaha would let me, once she agreed to get started."

"Ever climbed the Feather in that thing?" Sally asked.

"Nope."

"I'm not going to tow you if you get stuck, like that other time," said Sally, referring to an unfortunate incident down in the Delta when I'd neglected to study the tide tables.

"Won't need to. Got lots of gas. Plus a new altimeter. And my trusty depth finder clicked off depths like crazy all the way here. Me and mine are all set. You just lead the way, Sally. Keep me in two feet of water and I'll stay right in your tale."

The day before Sally Sturgeon and I headed upriver, a graveside funeral was held for my wife's aunt. Janie and I *sans* Sally attended the ceremony—it was held at the cemetery dead west of the City of Woodland, the one next to the Flyer's Club golf course, up on a gentle rise of a hill overlooking an otherwise flat plain of row crops and orchards and pasture. It's odd to be above the valley, being able to look down; Sally would have found it especially interesting. The orchards immediately south were of almonds, in full pink-white bloom. It rained felines and canines until just an hour before the ceremony. The broken blue sky made it pleasant for the friends and relatives in attendance.

The aunt had lived 45 years in Bryte, which disappeared in the late 1980's, merging with its sister Broderick into the City of West Sacramento. A jog of the neighboring Sacramento River remains Bryte Bend. The Bryte and Broderick twins were settled by Russian emigrants in the 1800's. The aunt is survived immediately by her husband and a bushel of kids and grandkids and great grandkids, decreasingly Russian. It's a large clan, as is Sally's. The aunt and her sister lived no more than a block apart their entire lives. Sally and her relatives are spread over gazillions of gallons, a hundred thousand square miles.

The dead aunt's sister is married to George. Uncle George, we call him. He used to own two bars. Sally's River owns a score or more, like the one at the mouth of the Feather. Uncle George sold the bars, laid off the sauce, and quit smoking cigars all at once, a few years back. He may have felt the aunt's death sneaking up on him. Though sturgeon drink a lot, they can not abide cigars; one problem is that they don't have any teeth: they can't bite off the cigar end as is the habit of *sapiens*. Uncle George may have quit smoking and drinking, but not the telling of true stories. He's a kin to Ossian—Sally's famous fish tale telling grand-daddy—in that regard.

Uncle George and I stood apart from the dead aunt's final gathering and he told me, again, about when he was young and the August Saturdays were hot, and he and a substantial proportion of the teenagers of Bryte would go down to the beach at Bryte Bend. Aside the levee that kept The River out of the town ran the Sacramento Northern Railroad, transporting various people and freight up and down the valley. On really hot August Saturday afternoons, Uncle George and the other boys would lie on the beach, listening for the whistle. *Freight train coming into town*, they'd yell, running up the levee to look. If they were right—if it wasn't a passenger train speeding for Woodland or Corning or beyond—they'd hop aboard and ride upriver to the watermelon and cantaloupe fields at Beatrice. Each of the boys would harvest two arm's full of the fat fruits (preferably the melons, they floated better than the cantaloupes, but the lopes would do in a pinch), skittdaddle back across the tracks and up the levee bank before the farmer in question happened by to ask one, and heave the fruits into The River. An hour later, Uncle George and the boys—like a flotilla of little tug boats—would appear around the corner of Bryte Bend, herding the gaggle of floating fruits from behind. They'd slice up the melons and the lopes river-cold for all the girls on the beach, hoping, of course, to make an impression. I don't know if that's how Uncle George met the sister of the just-dead aunt. When Sally heard this story, she commented that sturgeon don't care much for melons or lopes *per se*, but they sure do fancy the seeds.

Ossian had told Sally there'd once been a train wreck downriver from Uncle George's Bryte Bend, down near Garcia Bend where the tracks come up on the levee. Train full of watermelons pulled by a smoke belching steam engine heading down to Antioch, maybe to Crockett, to meet a ship, probably a three masted clipper, bound for points beyond. Train fell off the tracks, plop, into The River. A million (said Ossian) melons floated past Clarksburg. Became waterlogged at Courtland. Started sinking by Rio Vista. Were decomposing at Antioch. About the time the meloness passed Crockett, it was attacked by a swarm of sturgeon and was seedless by the Carquinez Strait.

The challenge to breeding like a green sturgeon when you're white is finding a good spot. A redd, it's called. Why whites do it in the Delta and greens do it upriver isn't the issue. Down in the Delta, where she'd done it before, there are so many anabranches, back streams, bayous, bights, burns, canals, channels, coves, cuts, cutoffs, ebbs, eddies, fluxes, guts, influents, inlets, logans, pokelogans, races, reaches, rivers, slews, sloughs, slues, streams, straits, watercourses and watersmeets (and, once, watermelons!) that finding a spot to *do it* is like pulling into Las Vegas and saying to your boyfriend, "Do you think we'll be able to find a room?"

She wasn't concerned about finding a white mate; someone was sure to come by, even way up the Feather. Sally wasn't concerned about *the act*; when a girl sturge gets the urge, the eggs just naturally start flowing. The boys do the rest.

We finally reached Oroville by foot and by fin. I had abandoned the pontoon boat and the inessential equipment and provisions above Marysville, where Honcut Creek joins the Feather. High water season or not, Sally tired of scouting through the morass of sandbars and sawyers and islands trying to find water two feet deep and six plus a little feet wide to accommodate my craft. I'd crammed my sleeping bag and the loaf of French bread into the plastic ice chest atop the beers, tied a rope to one of the handles, and dragged it behind me the last fifteen miles. It was actually much faster than the previous technique, and Sally was much happier. She got to nap when I lagged behind from slow crossings of land, tugging the ice chest weighted by two cases of Coors. We'd stopped every hour or so, when our paths crossed in the river. I would lighten the ice chest load by a can or two and lie on the sand while she recounted old Ossian stories, few of which were new to me.

Camp was set for the night on a spit of sand under the Highway 70 bridge on the north edge of town. The Feather gurgled and eddied steadily. The moon shimmered on the deep green ripples as an elongated orb of pure white, in anticipation. The coals of the campfire glowed dim red. Sally was asleep, just a few yards away on the bottom, safe beneath an outcropping of rock. Weary from the trek, soothed by the Feather, I joined Sally in her dreams of tomorrow.

I awoke to a great splashing of water. It was Sally, the glow of dawn above her. I crawled from my bag, peed against the concrete vertical bottom of the bridge, and sauntered down to the water's edge.

"Good morning Carpenter," said Sally.

"Good morning to you, miss sturgeon of the day. Hey, do you remember the Longfellow poem I read you a few months ago? The one about Hiawatha and his travails with Mische-Nahma, King of Fishes?"

"That's not a true tail, Carpenter. That sturgeon killing never really happened. "

"I know. It's just a *sapien* poem. It's not like an Ossian tale. But I was dreaming it when you splashed me awake. *Forth upon the Gitche Gumee, On the shining Big-Sea-Water.* I'd just gotten to the part where the sturgeon swallows Hiawatha <u>and</u> his canoe <u>and</u> his pal the squirrel. But I couldn't remember the squirrel's name."

"Adjidaumo."

"Yeah, that's it. It's an odd name, though Mische-Nahma's not too common either. Same with Ossian, I suppose."

"Carpenter, why do we have a tail of a squirrel and a dead lake sturgeon here in my story? This is *my* special day and I barely slept and I want to lay and I don't want to hear about any more stupid *sapien* poetry! "

"Sorry, sorry, sorry. Forget Longfellow and his critters and my dream. You barely slept?"

"Rolled and finned all night. My belly feels like it's going to explode. I've never mastered sleeping on my side. I always swallow water if I don't keep my mouth on the bottom. Wakes me up every time."

Myself, I never wake up at night. Except when Janie kicks me awake for snoring. I snore when I sleep on my back. And drink too much. Though Janie's taught me to be a pretty decent side-sleeper, now was not the time to share this anecdote with my best sturgeon friend.

"What's the itinerary for the day, Sally?"

"I'm not exactly sure," she said. "If we were back down in the Delta, I'd find a good slough—used Georgiana the first time, Potato the second, Three Mile for the third, and Montezuma last time—and just drop down to the bottom, start squirting 'em out. The boys would catch the scent and come, by and by. But we're going to have to experiment a little up here. Feel our way through it. Can you see any whites from up there?"

This was <u>not</u> an odd question, for sturgeon can't see worth a damn. They smell to find things. "Why don't I walk up the bank a ways and take a look," I offered.

"Find me a big handsome one," she teased.

I got up off my hands and knees, visited the ice chest, and headed up stream toward the dam at the Feather River Fish Hatchery. I'd been there before; it's a place where they manufacture steelhead and salmon. They slit open pregnant females for the eggs, masturbate some males for their juice, and stir the whole shebang together in a stainless steel tank. It's very crude. I would never tell Sally about it. I thought of inviting the hatchery folks to come watch her do it the natural way, but decided against it. They'd do something to screw it up, for sure. Damn *sapiens*.

About fifty yards below the dam I found them. Three whites. Knowing that you can not tell a male sturgeon from a female (unless they are in heat, bloated like Sally), I climbed down the bank and beckoned them over.

"Any of you boys?" I asked.

"Who are you? And how do you know how to talk?" one of them replied.

"Name's Carpenter. I'm a friend of Sally Sturgeon. She lives in Steamboat Slough, down in the Delta. She's up here to breed."

"Never heard of her, though I been through that slough before," said another, a big one, looked to be three hundred pounds.

"Her grand-daddy's named Ossian."

"*The* Ossian?" the third sturgeon asked.

"There's only one."

"Ossian's grand-daughter is up here wanting to get laid?"

"That's right. Her name is Sally," I said. "You guys or gals?"

"We three be males," said the big one. "Here on vacation. Don't hang out with the greens who live here though. Don't mess around with no greens, no sir."

"I thought the *sapien* said she was Ossian's kin," whispered the third sturgeon to the big one.

"Hey, Mr. Carpenter *sapien,* this Sally, she a white?" the big one asked.

"Yes sir," I said.

"What in Neptune's sake is a white doin' breeding up here? This is green country."

"Why don't you boys just drift down a few hundred yards and ask her," I suggested, rising to my feet and walking away. The hook had been set. Three boys from the Delta, and one of them a big hunker to boot, on vacation. White sex in a pool of greens. They'll squirt like fire hoses. Sally will be pleased, I thought.

I hurried back to camp to give Sally the news. She was close to shore, her swollen belly bottomed on the soft sand. She looked miserable.

"Oohh, Carpenter, I'm so ready. I'm gonna' burst. Ooohhh, I'm gonna lay any minute, I need a mate, I want a big white male right now, right now, ooohhhh."

"They're going to come here any minute," I said to Sally. "Hold on. Got you three, three big whites. You're going to love them. They're on the way."

"Are they nice boys?" Sally moaned.

"They're nice and they're from the Delta. I spoke with them. They'll love you." I stood up to see if my promise would be kept, and there they were, circling slowly out in the pool.

"The boys are here Sally. You're on your own. I'm going up the bank to get out of the way."

"Carpenter?"

"Yes Sally?"

"You can watch if you want," my good friend offered.

"I'd like that," I said.

Unsure of how long the event might take, I dragged the ice chest with me. It was a sight. It looked like love at first smell, though she was so ready to lay that a lost and down-trodden tuna might have prevailed upon her. Sally spat eggs from her belly like the bombing run over Dresden. The boys swarmed around them, shooting their stuff as the eggs sank to the bottom. Then Sally let loose again, and they did the same. None of them stopped for a rest, nobody took time off for lunch. The clear Feather water became milky with sperm. The rocky Feather bottom became coated with eggs. Sally came ten times, a hundred eggs each. The boys came until they could come no more. They drifted off downstream. Panting.

Sally and I headed home mid-afternoon. We stopped at the dredge tailings east of Biggs at nightfall. She went to sleep immediately, exhausted. A thousand coated eggs lay in the gravel bottom of the Feather behind us. Sixteen days, plus or minus, and the egg yolks would break, little Sallies wiggling free, rising to ride the current downstream at night, hiding on the bottom by day, towed to the safety of the Delta by the mother of it all, The River. Though few will make it, my bet's that there'll soon be more newcomers than usual downriver: those boys and Sally did it right. You should have seen it.

Were he alive, old Ossian would be so proud of his sagacious granddaughter that he'd probably construct a quite wonderful tale about our adventure. As for me, well, I can't wait to see the kids down at Steamboat Slough in the fall. I can't wait to tell them that I was there when they became.

STURGEON RIDERS

*T*hey showed themselves the first time. I'd been stealthed in the reeds of the bank, fishing. It was another moon-full night, the air wisped with the beginnings of a tule fog, and I'd leapt, startled, to gain a better look. That, of course, spooked them. Returning a dozen times to the same place, feigning the pursuit of midnight catfish and high-noon striped bass, I'd not seen them again. Until tonight.

The water in question would be called *slough* by the conventional occupants of the Delta: fish tackle, beer, and bait purveyors; retired and weather-beaten marina owners; pile-driving, clam-bucketing, channel-deepening barge operators; city-folk families on three-day weekend houseboat rental jaunts, nannies aboard; water skiers in search of the flat and solitary.

Slough by default, slough by habit, slough by omission; for there are eighty and more sloughs forenamed Babel, Barker, Beaver, Boynton, Broad, Cache, Champion, Connect, Cross, Cutoff, Deadman, Denverton, Dissapointment, Duck, Dutch, Elk, Fourteen Mile, French Camp, Frost, Gallagher, Georgiana, Howard, Indian, Italian, Kusal, Latham, Lindsey, Little Connection, Little Potato, Lookout, Lost, Luco, Mallard, Mayberry, Miner, Middle, Montezuma, New York, Norther, Noyce, Nurse, Peytonia, Piper, Potato, Prospect, Ridge Cut, Roaring River, Rock, Sacramento, Salmon, Sand Mound, Seven Mile, Shag, Sheep, Snodgrass, Steamboat, Suisun, Sutter, Sycamore, Taylor, The Meadows, Three Mile, Tom Paine, Tomato, Trapper, Volanti, Wells, Whiskey, White, Wilkens and the like in the Delta.

Jedediah Strong Smith, crossing the Sacramento Valley in search of beaver, 1828: "I was obliged to cross many *slous* of the River that were very miry. . .."

But *slough* this particular water is not.

Also not *creek*; for a creek is a watercourse that departs to a saltwater estuary on a low coast. Nor a *pokelogan*; for though my water appears somewhat stagnant and marshy, it is connected both above and below to its mother: the great Sacramento, unquestionably a *river*. It is not a *race, rapid, reach,* or *riffle*; a *rill, rindle, runnel,* or *rivulet*; a *flux,* a *ford,* or a *freshet; brook, brooklet,* or *burn.* Nor a *fall* or a *cascade,* a *pond* or a *lake.* It is not a *cove, firth, inlet, loch, lough, strait, gut, lagoon, harbor, basin, sound, bay, sea* or *ocean.*

It is, for it flows, a *stream.* But all moving waters are streams, so stream does not edify. It is close to a *bayou,* for it is sluggish and follows a tortuous course. Parts of it are a *meander,* though not right here.

Anabranch.

Like the Delta breeze, but twice daily, a salty current moves up through my anabranch from San Francisco Bay, hop-scotching the Bays of San Pablo and Suisun, battling the clear-water current spilled days before from Shasta Dam, a half-State north. When the insistence of these two currents balance, the watercourses between become immobile. Such is the case now. My anabranch is suspended, excepting a ripple prescient of the arrival of fish. I suspect it is their time.

On the bank across, movement begins: subtle and noiseless. Fuzzy brown tops of cattails sway slightly as their stalk bottoms are pressed aside. A sound like a snake's slither in tall grass trundles across the water. On the narrow mud shore, small translucent bodies appear: tail-less, four legged, eyes shining. Amid the anabranch, ripples rise from roiling sturgeon backs. Diamond plated, white-gray colored, a dozen or more each longer than the fishing pole beside me. Single file, the fish ease toward shore and are mounted, one on one, by members of the cluster on the bank. Friends assist in the task by wading out waist deep, steadying the fish, offering stubby arms of support. Though the riders and assistants look practiced, commotion reigns on the bank and in the shallow. One rider slides off his sturgeon-mate twice in the attempt to mount, and the shoreline silence is broken with chatter and cajoling. Those successful join the growing meander of fish-forms bobbing and idling in the middle of the anabranch. The final sturgeon-rider team draws the meander into a circle and the whole conglomeration begins to turn about, like a carousel.

On my anabranch, inside the spinning orb, an eddy forms. Froth and foam appear as flotsam on the outside wake. Wavelettes lap the watercourse banks.

Inside the gyrating orb, a whirlpool begins. Bantam breakers tumble the shoreline.

Twigs and leaves are drawn in.

The water dances whitecapped. Surges crash the tules. I am swept away, down into the vortex, floating entrapped but unharmed at the conical bottom, spinning slowly, looking up at sturgeon bellies, proboscis tubed mouths, quads of dangling barbel feelers teetering at the air-water edge of the cone, the riders atop it all, each leaning down toward me against the centrifugal force, waving and giggling as they whirl faster and faster, dropping me deeper into the waterless vacuum hole of a fish-formed, secret Delta maelstrom.

They slow. The vortex walls tilt back. The whirlpool flattens. The waves cease. I tread water. The fish and the riders circle once more, laughing, then spin off in single file, aimed upstream. *We're off for some fun*, they shout back over silver sturgeon tails. *Yippie-yi-oh-ki-a y e* , they yell into the moon-full night on the anabranch.

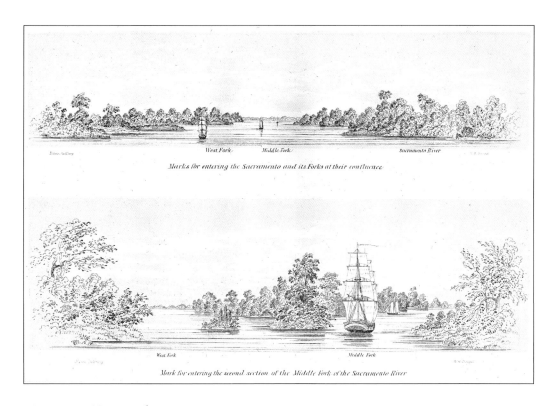

Marks for entering the Sacramento and its Forks at their confluence

Mark for entering the second section of the Middle Fork of the Sacramento River

THE TORNADO

"In o T h e r , oldEn times there were only
pHantoms.
In the beginNing, that iS.
IF there eVer was A beginniNg."

Henry Miller,
Big Sur and the Oranges of Hieronymus Bosch, 1957.

March 20 1996, Channel Three Six O'clock Evening News headline: Tornado in the Delta. The post-headline reporter retreated. "Tornado-like weather most of the afternoon," she said, as the shots of Tiki Lagùn, a marina west of Stockton, made their way from the camera in the helicopter back to the station and on to the screen of my television set, appearing as de-roofed boat docks, horizontal trees, sundry land-borne flotsam and jetsam, and a half-dozen half-sunk boats. "Similar damage has been reported at Bullfrog Landing and Turner Cut," she said, assuming I'd trust her without live footage. I clicked the quasi-tornado, delta weather report off.

And composed one of my own backyard: a north of the Delta, east bank of the Sacramento River, weather report. For most of the day up at my place, the sky had kaboom-kaboom-a-boomed, dropping felines and canines and flashy white streaks of electricity to the ground: drop, splatter, drip, splatter, shizboom. Damage report: two broken flower pots, glueable; a displaced ensemble of plastic patio furniture, replaceable; and one ripped-from-the-wooden-siding-of-the-house wisteria vine, replantable.

The fishpond outside the kitchen window looked like a helicoptered camera shot of Tiki Lagùn in miniature. The surface was congested with debris: twigs, leaves, and berries from the adjacent trees; an errant tennis ball; a woven straw placemat. A score or more of garden worms floated, light pink dead. Anxious about the pond's intentional occupants, I netted the storm's junk away and looked in. Ossian and Winslow, the little sturgeon twins, looked fine.

They were swimming figure-eights across the slightly trapezoidal bottom like it was a clear-water, summer day. Their nine koi pond mates were lurking, as usual, under the modest waterfall down at the end where the used-brick fireplace begins its ascent skyward into a chimney.

Pond and occupants all accounted for, I slogged across the backyard and down the ramp to the dock floating on the Sacramento, intent on bailing the sky water from the ski boat tied alongside. To my surprise—for she usually only comes upriver from her place on Steamboat Slough to visit on Sundays—there was Sally Sturgeon.

"Hey Carpenter, how are my boys?" Sally asked. She'd adopted the habit of calling them that soon after they'd moved in with Janie (she's my wife) and me, even though they weren't hers (they were born in captivity via arti-fishal means) and they might both be girls (for as Sally well knew, no one—*Acipenser* or *sapien*—can tell a male sturgeon from a female sturgeon from their outside appearance).

"They're fine. I just tidied up their place. They're cruising on the bottom as usual. Storm didn't seem to bother them a bit."

"Hell of a mess down in the Delta," Sally said. "Slivers and chunks of *sapien* structures are lying about the slough bottoms everywhere. Some sturge or catfish or striped bass is gonna bump that stuff and get cut up bad, if they aren't careful."

"Saw the conflagration on the television news myself. Said it was a tornado," I said.

At that, Sally got an odd look on her face and plunged under. A big stream of bubbles popped the surface. Then another. Then she was back.

"What's with all the bubbles?" I asked. "Never saw you exhale like that before."

"I was laughing," said Sally.

"You were laughing?"

"I was laughing."

"I didn't know that sturgeon could laugh,' I said, truly astounded.

"Usually not much to laugh *about,* Carpenter," Sally replied. "Like we've talked before, most of my days, and the days of most of my friends, are spent avoiding sturgeon slaughter at the hands of your *sapien* relatives. But Holy carp! A Tornado? Here in our Delta? Your Tornado line really rattled my barbels."

I tried to explain to Sally that I was a little surprised at the appearance of "tornado-like weather" myself. The fact that it made the evening news proved how unusual such a weathering was for the Delta, I said. She's never seen the six o'clock news, or anything on television for that matter, on account of her terrible eyesight. But Sally would have none of it.

"My grand-daddy—Neptune bless that dear old *Acipenser*—would be finning on his back, dorsal in the silt, belly to the sky, if he was here to hear you talk such nonsense, Carpenter. There has been only one Tornado. It happened way back in piscine antiquity, and there's never been the need for another since. Never will be. *That* Tornado got it all done, once and for all."

The mention of her grand-daddy, old Ossian (one of the two youngsters in my pond is named after him; the second is named after Ossian's father, Winslow, as is Marty the Artist's kid; it's confusing, I know) meant only one thing: Sally was about to share one of Ossian's famous fish tales. Anticipating a long one, I retrieved my high-tech sturgeon listening device from the dock. (The device allows me to avoid lying on my belly and getting an ear full of water when Sally comes by for a chat. It is a large blue plastic funnel duct-taped to a chunk of garden hose.) I pulled a mottled canvas captain's chair to the dock's edge, floated the funnel upside down on The River's surface, held the hose to my head's ear, and settled in for the duration. "It'll be dark in an hour," I said. "I want to feed the boys and the kois before dark, so start tailing."

When I finally got back to the house, a half-moon was reflecting from the darkened pond top. I turned on the underwater pond light and grabbed the two cartons of fish pellets: floaters for the koi, sinkers for the sturgies. The herd of koi were bunched in the middle treading water, mouths tilted toward the surface in anticipation of their evening meal of Koroabi (made in Japan) brand, medium size, guaranteed to not cloud the pond water, twelve dollars a pound, floating koi pellets. I tossed them a half of a handful. They attacked without hesitation. The surface boiled with an alternation of open mouths rising and tails, briefly airborne, sinking. The pond became an underwater amusement park, the koi riding an invisible Ferris Wheel exactly as tall as the pond was deep. When the final floating pellet was gone from the surface, the kois got off the ride, closed the twig turnstile, and flipped the little leaf that hung beside it from RIDE OPEN to RIDE CLOSED. Three of the koi then swam to the shallow end where the carousel ride was still in operation. Head to tail, tail to head, they took a few spins. When they too moved to the safety of the water-fall, I knew the koi dinner and amusement park had closed for the evening.

The two baby sturgeon stayed at it: the perpetual perfection of bottom hugging figure-eights. I tossed them a dozen Wardley (of Secaucus, New Jersey) brand sinking pellets. Sinkers from New Jersey, floaters from Japan—fish food the world over is made the same: chicken feet and sugar beet tops and sardine entrails and moldy soybeans and a variety of missing ingredients pulverized and mixed in tall, diesel powered Waring Blenders manned by underpaid and un-degreed food scientists.

The back panel of the sturgeon's made-in-New Jersey feed notes under the bold heading of GUARANTEED ANALYSIS: minimum crude protein 20%; minimum crude fat 3.5%; maximum crude fiber 2%; maximum moisture 8%. Allowing that the food scientists aren't lying, the two maximums total only ten percent.

Which leaves the sturgeon with two gastronomic options. Either the crude protein and crude fat numbers are way understated and need to be more than tripled to get the count up to 100, or there is approximately 66.5 percent of missing ingredients, or maybe a combination of missing ingredients—like carbohydrates, worm farm tailings, rose hips, tractor tires, vitamins, and polyvinylchloride—which the operators of the giant Waring Blenders are unwilling to disclose or discuss.

The fact that the sinking pellets <u>do so</u> indicates one thing: a bunch of the missing 66.5 is way heavier than water.

My sturgeon—like all sturgeon—have terrible eyesight. They couldn't read the back panel of the Wardley container with binoculars. Sally tried it once when she heard about the missing ingredients and grew concerned for the boys' health, but to no avail. When I read off the GUARANTEED ANALYSIS, she refused to taste even one of the sinking pellets. She prefers a natural diet of clams and ghost shrimps.

My koi—like most fish—can see pretty good, as evidenced by their run-to-the-waterfall habit when I come by to check out the pond. Koi are an example of what The Professor calls "modern fish."

Sturgeon smell great. The Professor once told me that when herring spawn down in San Francisco Bay, sturgeon from miles around pick up the scent and flock to the breeding grounds for a feeding frenzy. The Professor reminds us that sturgeon are "ancient fish."

Sturgeon also feel really well. That's what the four barbels are for. Barbels are like the whiskers on catfish, though with sturgeon they're located on the bottom, not the front, dangling about half way between the bow of the sturgeon (where the nose holes are) and the vacuum cleaner-like entrance to the sturgeon's tummy (it's called the proboscis).

The Professor once published an aquaculture book solely based on my recollection to him of Sally's explanation of how sturgeon combine smell and feel to eat. I believe he got tenure at the University because of Sally. In brief, the trick to successful sturgeon bottom feeding is this: smell, sense, suck. Sturgeon have survived since the Jurassic era, 200 million years ago, in part because the three vital tools are lined up morphologically correct: nose first, barbels second, proboscis third. Plus they are really, really, really intelligent, what with 200 million years of learn-by-doing coded into their 240 chromosomes. Once in a while, an *Acipenser* (like Sally) can talk. Less often, a *sapien* (like me) learns to be good listener.

As it turned out, the tornado tale didn't come from Ossian, only through him. Ossian heard it from Winslow, Sally's great grandfather. Knowing that sturgeon can live to be over a hundred, we figure he could have heard the tornado tale as a youngster in the late 1700's. From whom we'll never know.

Sally's daughter Arlene once suggested that Winslow had heard (remember the poor eyesight) a rough draft of The *Origin of the Species* straight from Charles himself, and sorta mixed up the Darwinian facts with some *Acipenser* humor. I reminded Sally that Darwin didn't write his tome until 1859, so that Arlene's hypothesis was unlikely, though a heck of a try for a slightly-schooled thirty year old. Sturgeon as a specie hold Darwin in high regard because of the aquatic flavor of his work (the *H.M.S. Beagle* and all).

There's no doubt in my mind that the tornado tale originated back in piscine antiquity. Clearly, it had to be after the page in Mother Nature's script where the ancient fish—the sturgeon, the paddlefish and the shark—were asked to stay behind while modern fish and the amphibians took a turn at the evolution game. Most likely it was three or four pages later, after The Mother sent some of the amphibians on to become birds and others to be mammals. (Like Sally often says: "Carpenter, remember that sturgeon are *your* parents too.") But worrying about *who* crafted the tale is like worrying about which *sapien* named all the constellations, created the zodiac, and authored our own fables therefrom. At some point, you decide it really doesn't matter. You swallow the whole collection of stuff as is, kit and caboodle.

The tone of the tornado tale is constrained by the shape of the sturgeon's watery world, as well as their historically poor eyesight. Theirs is a world of three dimensions. We *sapiens* are boxed in by two, no matter what your third grade science teacher told you. We can only go over and across under our own power, not up (down can be, on occasion, a different matter). Sturgeon not only go over and across, but up and down too. The "down" does have a bottom—it's *the bottom*—and the "up" has a top: right where the aqueous terminates and the gaseous initiates. The sturgeon's top is a line nearly infinitely thin: the width of nothingness between the highest edge of the tippy-toppest water molecule and the lowest edge of a nitrogen, or an oxygen, maybe a helium, could be a carbon dioxide—whatever gas molecule happens to be there at the time.

Sapiens too have a top, but it is diffuse and ephemeral; we are in it, and we can see above it, and (because of rocket ships) we can look down on it, and it goes on maybe forever and ever. The *sapien's* top is nearly as infinitely thick as the sturgeon's is thin.

Because of their environment, the sturgeon's mythology turned out different from ours. With few exceptions, they know of *nothing* above the water line.

Because of these cognitive constraints (and, admittedly, the fact that there are a few sturgeon words I haven't learned to translate), what *Somesturgeon* told Winslow's predecessors to tell old Winslow to tell Ossian the tale-teller to tell Sally to tell me to tell you may be hard to fathom. I assure you that Sally did the best she could; that's her way. I can't speak for the others.

Long before *Somesturgeon* lived, someone had separated the earth into solids, liquids, and gases, and named the constituents land, water, and air.

Less long before *Somesturgeon,* the land had busied itself shooting off volcanoes, sliding continent-sized pieces of the earth's crust around on tectonic plates, and sprouting a modest collection of ferns, bushes, moss, and the like. The air had mostly just rested, allowing the plants on the land to alter its composition, oxygen-wise. Most of the water had settled into the seas, as had all of the animals. Every first one. Of these, the ancient fish (the *Chonodrostei*) were the wisest and biggest. Out of this family, Mische-Nahma hand-picked *Somesturgeon* to be schooled in the talents of watching and telling. This is about where Sally's version of the events begins, with Mische-Nahma and the ancient fish, maybe 200 million years or so ago, back in the time called The Jurassic.

Mische-Nahma was princess of the ancient fishes. She was young and beautiful.

Longfellow named the sturgeon in his Hiawatha poem for her, much like I named the backyard pond-mates Ossian and Winslow after more recent members of the ancient fish family. It seems that great names hold up for a long time.

Ancient fish back then were of various shapes (nearly everything except square) and just short of an infinite number of sizes (small as a gnat, big as six Moby Dicks). The sea was also filled with lots of other animal types, some of whom survive looking nearly identical today, most of whom passed into extinction through the whim of Mother Nature. But of all the sea's critters, the ancient fishes were clearly on the cutting edge of aquatic life. They had multiple senses. They could move. They reproduced well (albeit slowly; even modern sturgeon wait until their mid-twenties to breed, and then do so only every eight years).

Neptune was the god-king of the sea (he still is). He was bigger and more powerful in the ways of nature than Mische-Nahma, his underling. Neptune hung out with the god-kings of the other realms: land and air. They all, of course, worked for The Mother, who reported to the Big God (the one who created our universe). It's not clear who the Big God worked for; the ancient fish never considered it. In fact, *Somesturgeon* stopped knowing about these things right at the Mische-Nahma level. Who gave *her* the orders was none of his concern.

Every millennium or so, the three god-kings met for lunch at some mutually agreeable interface of the three realms. The possibilities were, as you can imagine, limited. The air god-king was pretty easy going about this, for he covered both land and sea and had only to parachute to the bottom of his realm, aimed at wherever it met both of the others. The land god-king was touchy about where lunch was to be held, for though he controlled the smaller of the earth's two surfaces, the watery edges of his lands were considerable in length. Four, five continents (it depended on which day the lunch was held) each with a sea edge, and more rivers, brooks, streams, rills, rivulets, sloughs and anabranches (each with two sides!) than the Big God had galaxies. If the luncheon location was insufficiently specified, Land was sure to be late; he'd still be running along a bank or shore, searching, while the others were finishing the first course, wiping. One time he didn't arrive until dessert; he'd been looking for lunch on the wrong continent. He was generally grumpy anyway, for there was not much doing upon the lands. Sure, a late-to-blossom volcano might sporadically spout—fire up the air, maybe roll shiny orange lava hissing into the sea—but nothing and nobody was moving around on land except the plants. And they moved slowly. Very slowly.

The three had once held a luncheon where the land and the sea met vertically. It was a poor choice. Neptune and Land had to yell up and down the cliff to make the other hear, and poor Air—always getting the worst of it—had to bounce up and down to follow the conversation. Plus, Air was quite poor at hearing. There was nothing *in* air to make a noise back then, other than occasional thunder or the sound of Neptune's water raining back on itself. For Air, every sound (other than the threesome's once in a millennium lunch conver-sation) was an echo of a peer's past actions, so he hadn't had much to practice with. It was quiet in the air. Very quiet.

The current lunch was at the edge of an estuary of a bay at the end of a great river. Air and Land were whining, as usual, about their mutual problems. Neptune sipped his wine, nodding occasionally, feigning empathy. It seemed to him that the lunches had been going on like this forever.

"Can't you spare just a *few* critters to accompany my plant life?" Land pestered Neptune, for what must have been the tenth time in the last million years.

"No way," said the sea god, "not until you get that volcanism completely out of your system. Someone could get hurt."

Air took a different approach. "Hey Nepper, how about a couple of flying fish to break-up the monotony? I'm bored with the incessant drizzle, the afternoon breezes. How about it, old buddy?"

"Maybe in a few million," said Neptune. "But not until The Mother finds a good reason why fish should start flying." His voice remained controlled. He held himself above all this squabbling. He was king of the best of the three realms, after all, and he was not about to squander the advantage.

As was protocol, Mische-Nahma sat just behind Neptune at the table, politely following the interchanges. (There were comparable assistants behind land and air too, but Ossian couldn't recall their names or titles.) Mische-Nahma had always been faithful and true to her boss, carrying out his every whim as to her charge—the ancient fishes. Most of her days were spent on the tedious task of slow and steady evolution; a longer fin here, wider gills there, add a tooth, drop a scale. All this work left little time for her favorite of the ancients: the sturgeon. They had settled into adequate form and function long before, and were now working on tuning their cognitive abilities. Helping with this was a lot of fun for Mische-Nahma. Teaching *Somesturgeon* how to take notes and how to remember was especially rewarding. Fussing with the other ancient fish's morphology and physiology was a pain; it was so tedious that she'd nearly quit the job with Neptune & Company three times in just the last twenty million years. It wasn't very exciting even when the word came down from The Mother through Neptune to do a termination. You didn't just make a whole specie go *poof;* even those things took years, often dozens of thousands.

So Mische-Nahma daydreamed away the decades between each god-king word, wondering how she'd ever get ahead in this world, glancing occasionally at the other assistants for hints of their feelings on the same, tapping her foot, fidgeting in her seat. And it hit her.

One day, after that luncheon (a long time, or a short time after, Ossian didn't know), Mische-Nahma appeared at Air's front door and asked for an appointment. To do so was not necessarily suspect, for she was often sent on errands to the air and land god-king's places, but it was a little unusual. After a while (an hour or a millennia, Ossian wasn't sure), Air admitted her to his inner chamber.

"What's up, Mische?" he said.

"I had a thought during the last god-king lunch."

"That's terrific, MN. Had a thought, did you? That's just great. So what?"

"I have a proposition which might be of interest to you, oh great god of the air," she replied.

"This an idea from your boss, that pompous Neptune?"

"No sir. It's my own. May we speak in confidence?"

"He know you're over here?"

"No sir. And he'd Ahab-me for sure if he ever found out. I have come to you at great personal risk. With an original idea that's time, I believe, has come."

"I didn't know you lesser gods were allowed to have original ideas. Oh man, is *my* lackey trippin-out like you?"

"I can not say whether she is or is not, oh great lord and master of the emptiness above sea and land."

"Don't say *emptiness* around here, you little scamp. I abhor the word and each and every of its relatives. Void. Deficient. They all make me want to puke."

"My point exactly, oh wise one of the atmosphere," she said. "Your realm is just that, and it's due to the greed of the sea king, under whom I slave millennia after millennia, unappreciated, unrespected, underpaid. I need to get ahead in this game of life, so I've decided to dump the old frump."

"Hey Mische, cool it on the Neptune trashing. Me and old Nep and that dreary land guy are in this earth thing together, through thick and thin. Now, I've got stuff to do, so if you'll excuse me . . ."

"Hear me out, sparkling bright sky-god of the star-filled heavens! I can fill your pristine void with a most beautiful animal, if you'll allow it."

"Allow it? Why, I'd trade a sky awash with ruby-filled meteors for a permanent resident in my airs. What sort of animal?"

"An animal avian, sir. I believe Mother Nature has reserved the word *bird* for this creature. We could call it so, if that pleases you."

"Take a seat, you sweet little fishie. Tell me more."

Sometime later, the god-king of land was awakened from an ice age long nap by the pounding on his castle door. He'd been dreaming of ferns with feet and tree trunks that could roll, self-propelled, across the inanimate and dreary surface of his realm. "Who is it?" he yelled.

"It is I, oh lord of the land. Mische-Nahma."

"Who?" said land, still groggy and, as usual, grumpy.

"Mische-Nahma, princess of the ancient fishes."

"The rapscallion who works for Neptune?"

"Yes it is I, though your slander offends me and I shall take leave if you do not open the gates and admit me at once."

"I offend you? Open at once? Why, I'm of a mind to send my junior goddess to the home of the watery old codger and report your behavior right now!" roared the god-king.

"Hear me out, oh great lord of the Himalayas, master of the plains, grower of ferns."

"Don't you say *ferns* to me, you waif. I'm so tired of green that I've considered re-lighting the volcanoes and torching the whole place. Melt the ice caps, flood the whole friggin planet and be done with it. The future seems so aqueous anyway. I don't know why I even bother."

"Hear me out, oh angry but sage one. I have brought you a great gift."

"Don't need no gift. I've got mountains of precious metals and gems piled high into my friend the air-god's sky. Go away, you presumptuous piscine hag. Let me get back to sleep."

"It is a special gift, oh great god of the fertile but unfruited plains. It is an idea."

"What *idea*?"

"A way to cover your grounds with moving animals."

"There are no such things, you water-logged, kelp-sucking nitwit. All the animals live in the sea, under the protection of that fat and ungracious god—god! huhh!—who calls himself Neptune. King of the sea, my ass."

"Hear me out, oh spiteful man of the mountains. Think of it: animals on four legs— maybe, someday, on two—running across the landscape, climbing your trees, digging in the soil you have spent these last millions of millennia to create. Think of it!"

"These animals, will they be fornicators?"

"We can work out the details. Interested?"

"Come on in, little darlin'. Come on in," cackled the god of the land.

Sally had dived to gill oxygen six times during the tornado tale telling, and had been down this last time for half an hour. Maybe she was snacking on a clam or a crawdad. I was dying for a tuna sandwich and a cold Budweiser myself, but I didn't want to leave the dock on The River for fear I'd miss the end of Ossian's tale. When she surfaced, I spoke before she could start again.

"Sally, you sure you've got that last part right?" I asked.

"Ossian said that's what Winslow told him, Carpenter."

"The land guy actually called Mische-Nahma a kelp-sucking nitwit?"

"That's how the tail goes, Carpenter."

"How do the sturgeon feel about such name-calling? Isn't Mische-Nahma a heroine to your specie?"

"Look Carpenter, I'm telling you the tornado tail as true as I can, cross my gizzard and hope to drown. I'm not going to make any judgments on the ancients."

"Well, what happened next?"

"We're getting to the best part, actually. You'll soon see why I thought it so funny that you believed the moronic television bitch."

Oh my goodness, there she goes again. I'd tried to enroll her in charm school last year, but she'd refused. But I couldn't let this behavior pass un-noticed, so I said, sternly: "Sally, we've talked about your language before. The gal on Channel Three was just reporting the facts as she knew them. You shouldn't call her a bad name like *moron* just because of a little misinterpretation of the weather. What would my *sapien* friends think if they were to hear you?"

"Don't care what they'd think. If I had my way, I'd tell your fellow *sapiens* what Mische-Nahma eventually told all three of the male schmucks in the ancient times: *fuck you*."

Oh my, oh my. She is riled up. "Does Mische-Nahma say *that* in the tornado tale?" I asked.

"Not in my grand-daddy's version. She probably thought it; she was a great fish woman, way ahead of her times ."

"And so are you. You're quite the vamp, if you don't mind me saying so, miss Sally Sturgeon. Like the time you bred up in the Feather River instead of the sloughs of the Delta. Every *Acipenser transmontanous* in The River was talking about that one!"

"My fellow white sturgeon are pretty fond of gossip, it's true. We got a big head start over most other critters thanks to Mische-Nahma, once she was free of Neptune's direct control. Back before The Tornado, he was forever ordering her to modify the piscine physical. But she was bored with that. He said it was the way of The Mother, and ordered her to quit griping and stick to the proven and sure path. But it's so slow, she'd complain, and there's so many animals in the sea, she'd tell him. Step by step, he'd always reply, that's the way of evolution, them's The Mother's orders. Physical evolution drove Mische-Nahma nuts; she was much more interested in schooling her favorite fishes—we sturgeon—on the intellectual. The disagreement with the sea god over brain versus brawn is what eventually led to the mutiny."

"*Somesturgeon* was Mische Nahma's secret study," Sally continued. "It took one-on-one tutoring for centuries, but she finally succeeded. He learned how to observe and he learned how to remember, all in preparation for the big day. Mische-Nahma wanted someone she could trust to pass along to all the future sturgeon how life came out of the ocean into the other two realms—the ones we can not see, not even today; the ones above the top of our world, above the waterline."

"Well, what happened after she visited the two whining god-kings?"

"Ossian said that when The Tornado finally came, all heck broke loose, that's what. Neptune was livid, he went berserk. You would have thought that he'd time-traveled into an apparition of Captain Ahab, hooked to you know who. Now there was a fish that I'd like my children to role model! Anyway, Neptune played right into the hands of the crafty fish goddess. And *Somesturgeon* took notes.

So it was that the greatest scam of the Jurrasic was set to motion by the three conspirators. The land god was delegated the task of locating Neptune and delivering a message. This wasn't easy, for the king of the sea spent most of his time in his grotto, counting and recounting the earth's critters, all of which were aqueous and his. Land finally found him one afternoon napping in the shallows of a marsh near the Island of Calafia.

"What do *you* want?" said Neptune, awakened by the approach of Land.

"Why do you think I always *want* something, great lord of the seas? I'm only here to announce the location of the next luncheon; it's my turn to pick, as you might recall, and I have a real treat in store for you and Air."

"You're not here to grovel for a favor, whine again about the lack of moving things in your flat, brown realm?"

"Why no! And my land is not all brown, it is populated with wonderful green plants and mosses. I just love all that greenness. I have turned over a new leaf: no more complaining from me, oh wise owner of all the animals of earth. In fact, I have a present for you, as I tried to mention at the outset."

"You have a present for me?" asked Neptune, skeptical of his peer's intentions, as always.

"We are going to lunch at the North Pole!"

"You second-rate, lord of the dirt idiot, that can't possibly be! The top of our orb is covered with *ice;* and ice is water, liquid or not. Where would *you* sit?"

"Not a problem. Lunch won't be served for another ten thousand years, so I've got plenty of time to slide a few continents and islands around to clear the ice. And there's a big chunk of nearly pure iron that's been bumping around the sea bottom forever; well, at least since The Mother put me in charge of solids. The thing has been a real nuisance. I thought I'd park it up at the North Pole as long as I was going to the trouble to modify the local geography for lunch. We can sit on it. What do you think?"

"Might be a nice change of scenery," said Neptune, feeling even loftier than usual from the presentation of a gift by a supplicant. "Is Air agreeable to this?"

"Air don't care, you know him. He can drop by anywhere, anytime," said the lord of the flat and dry.

"I accept your invitation. About time I got something from you besides a complaint. But it better be ice-free up there—you know how I detest the feel of solid water. Let my assistant Mische-Nahma know when you nail down the date; she'll put it on my calendar."

"Who's that again, Neptune?" queried Land.

"You know, the princess of the fishes. The gal who sits behind me at the lunch table."

"Oh, yes, I think I know the one you mean. I'll tell her. I'm sure she'll take care of everything. Yes, I'm quite sure of that."

Land set about to his tectonic task. It was a piece of cake. Heck, he'd split whole continents in two before; dug a hundred deep-sea trenches as abysmal as the Himalayas were aerial; made thousand-cubic-mile glaciers attack and recede the land like a ping-pong game. He'd defrosted the two polar ice boxes—and then promptly refilled them with god-sized ice cubes—so many times that an observer on another planet might have concluded that the sole activity on earth was a continuous cocktail party. He'd once spun some islands around so fast that it had made The Mother dizzy.

In no time at all, the top of the earth was nothing but clear, blue water, interrupted only by a single protruding chunk of iron. Waves lapped its edges quietly, for, as always, the kingdom of the air god was still vacant of life.

Many ancient fishes swam near, some bumping the newly arrived rock out of inexperience, but none of the these were sturgeon. In fact, the seas and oceans, bays and coves, and firths and fjords of the world seemed suddenly and conspicuously absent of the greatest of the ancients. None of the other fishes were intelligent enough to do more than take pause about this, but Neptune was more than just curious. He had planned to be down in his grotto grabbing a quick thousand year nap, as was always his habit prior to the luncheon. Instead, he was forced to stomp around his realm looking in all the crooks and crannies for the cream of the crop of his collection of critters, and they were nowhere to be found. Neither was the princess of the ancient fishes—his chief flunky, Mische-Nahma. Neptune hated losing a single animal, not to mention a whole species. This, and the lack of sleep, made him very cranky, but it was nearly time for lunch so he headed north.

He was the first to arrive. He paced around the fringe of the rock, waiting for the others, alternately fretting about the (hopefully temporary) low head count of his aquatic herd, and congratulating himself on his supreme dominance of all the earth's animals. Tired to the bone, he sat to the table—which was already set with the usual cutlery, cute blue-green napkins with little waves woven in, some odd looking snacks and a dozen carafes of strong wine—and propped up his feet, poured himself a tumbler, and popped a something or other into his gullet. Late again, damn those slacker gods of the air and the land, he thought. And damn those missing sturgeon. Another tumbler full, and then another.

Neptune awoke chilled to the bone, his head on his arms, his arms on the table. He opened one eye and saw white. Still dreaming, he thought. He opened another and saw white again. He wanted to see blue. He couldn't. He lurched up, knocking over the heap of now empty wine containers, and slowly turned in a circle. Ice. Everywhere. Ice. He was trapped.

Meanwhile, back at the equator, phase two of the great plan was proceeding nicely, though it was not a pretty sight. Fish were flying everywhere. Tornadoes by the thousands were hovered along the coastlines, sucking aquatic animals up and out of the water like gargantuan Hoovers of a later era. The god-kings of air and land were teamed in ultimate synchronicity, producing tornadoes as big as the Galapagos Islands like an assembly line at Henry Ford's Model T factory. As soon as one tornado would run out of steam and drop a billion fish on the places where water lapped land, the boys would spin up another. All the while, Mische-Nahma and her sturgeon charge were hiding in a secreted bay where—and this was no coincidence—the wind blew not at all. And all the same while, Neptune's teeth chattered in the cold, his only warmth created by the red-hot anger boiling in his belly. As the millennia passed, all the shores became cluttered with heaps of dying fish, dead fish and decomposing fish. Except every once in a while.

Every once in a while, one fish's fins grew stubby little fingers; another fish's gills figured how to process oxygen without needing water; yet another fish's tail rounded out, shrunk in diameter, and elongated. All the while, Mische-Nahma held the sturgeon in the safe place and passed the time teaching them new tricks and new talents of the intellect. And all the same while, Neptune's fury grew; he knew he'd been had.

When nearly every ancient fish in the sea (except, of course, you know who) had been sucked up high and plopped on the seashore, Air and Land moved the tornadoes inland and the plan into phase three. Mische-Nahma taught calculus and poetry. Neptune sat still, defeated. Birds appeared in the air. "Hooray!" yelled Air to his buddy land. Hairy, four-pedaled things that laid each other instead of eggs began roving across the land, eating and climbing the vegetation. "Yippie!!" yelled Land, immediately setting to the task of partially thawing the polar ice boxes so his new tenants wouldn't catch a chill in the dawns of mornings bright.

Thus was Neptune released from his prison of ice and snow, and thus did he make his way south, vengeance in his eyes, thoughts of the death of his once-trusted assistant, the ignoble princess of the ancient fishes, in his mind. South toward the equator went Neptune, across a sea barren of fish. When he first hit the shallows where water met land, he confronted things alive but not piscine. "What in Poseidon's sake are you?" he asked the frog, the crocodile, and the others. They, of course, didn't answer. He kept southward, already savoring the long and tortuous death he'd planned for the fish princess. He bumped a whale, a beluga. What the heck? he thought, but didn't bother to verbalize. He kept southward, now fantasizing in the extreme of the pleasure of his revenge of the back-stabbing assistant.

Neptune's search for the sturgeon was incessant. He paused neither for sleep nor sustenance. The orifice of every river was explored; the bottoms of deep ocean trenches examined; coral atolls were trolled; creeks, brooks, streamlets, rivulets, and springs were visited. A thousand years went by, yet his fervor never waned, so strong was his lust for Mische-Nahma's death, so huge was his phantasm of self-importance as King Of The Sea and master of all the animals of the earth. Emaciated, maniacal, blood thirsty, crazed. . .

. . . he found them, Mische-Nahma in their center, pedagoging on the talents of talking to *sapiens.* Raising his many, scaly extuberances above his vanity-swollen head, blood running oily hot, heart brimming with hatred, molten snot issuing from his sixteen nostrils, mind intent on death, lungs hyperventilating with anticipation—he plunged toward her position, scattering the ancient fishes from their school like gnats, slashing and maiming those who would not remove from his path, and faced her at long last. *"You are to die,"* he screamed with a voice that sent tidal waves smashing across all the continents and islands of the earth, as he careened forward to complete the deed, to repair his humiliation, to savage the perverter of all that was once his and his only.

But was halted in his tracks by a voice from the side, a voice he knew only too well.

"Stop," said the voice.

"Why?" said Neptune, his body throbbing with a million, billion angry cells each individually intent on the absolute annihilation of the fish princess.

"Don't you lay a hand on her."

"Huh?" said Neptune's mouth, though the rest of him had not yet ceased arching toward the target.

"She's been promoted. She is now Queen of the Fishes. She's your peer."

"Queen?" said Neptune's mouth, his brain now connected, the realization of The Mother's seriousness settling in.

"She did one heck of a job speeding up the development of this insignificant little world of land, air and water out in this no-where corner of my Universe. Heck of a job. I'm glad she showed some initiative. Frankly, Neptune, had you had your way, we would have never got the orb off the ground. I'm proud of her, and so's the Big God. He told me so yesterday."

"The Big God is siding with this traitorous wench?"

"Watch your tongue, old man. I've said my piece, and the deal is done. Now go away. There are still a few fish in the sea. Some interesting ones, actually; by-products of the tornado. Like that whale you ran into. Real nice guy. I think you'll like his specie. Go on, get outta here."

"And that's why I bubbled with laughter, Carpenter," said Sally. "Won't ever be another tornado; there's no need. The air above where we sturgeon live is already filled with flying things, and the land adjacent is covered with the likes of you, plus some other critters. At least, that's the sturgeon's folklore. But how would we know? For sturgeon, the world stops at the top of the water. And we couldn't see above it even if we wanted to. We've got terrible eyesight, you know."

Terrible eyesight indeed. I smiled and shook my head. "Sally, you can see *me*. And you're pretty handy with some other senses. You smell well and you're pretty good at the telling of tales, I should say."

"Now don't you start on me again, Carpenter. Every single word of The Tornado tail is true; my grand-daddy Ossian *told* me so."

"Goodnight, Sally Sturgeon. I've got to go feed the boys and the kois now."

"Night, Carpenter. Give the boys a hug and a kiss for me."

And that's when I went up the hill, crossed the lawn, and turned on the underwater light in the little fish pond next to my kitchen window, where the koi were soon riding the Ferris wheel operated by their baby sturgeon pondmates: the current generation of a line of interesting ancient animals that began even before *Somesturgeon* learned to listen and watch and take good notes.

HOW THE STURGEON GOT NEW FRIENDS

Sally Sturgeon's relatives go back 200 million years, give or take. Back to the time of the ancient fishes. The Jurassic, some famous *homo sapien* scientist called it.

Sally's relatives with remembered first names only go back a few hundred. Back to Winslow, her great grandfather. Sally never met him, though he was a legend even in his own time, according to his son Ossian. Ossian died in 1950 at the tender age of ninety. Died telling a story, they say. Ossian the famous fish tail teller, they still call him.

Sally says that Ossian told her that Winslow once explained that back in his early days there was nothing else piscine in The River. Nothing but white sturgeon *(Acipenser trans-nontanus,* some famous *homo sapien* scientist called them) like Winslow and his relatives. Then one day things changed, and the sturgeon got some new friends.

Ossian told Sally that Winslow was over to Snodgrass Slough when it started. Winslow was lying on the silt bottom, napping contentedly, when it began raining like crazy. Raining cats and dogs, as *homo sapiens* would say.

Napping contentedly until the first feline startled the water, *fwoopp*. A flock of canine followed—*sploch-sploch . . . sploch . . . sploch-sploch-sploch*—sending wavelets against the muddy muskrat-holed banks. And then it was cats and dogs all at once, a staccato of *fwoopps* and *sploches* creating raining-cats-and-dogs tidal waves that rushed over the peat berms, washing high-tide marks from trees lining the banks. *What's up?* wondered Winslow, suddenly fin deep in two specie of dead and drowning mammal.

When the downpour desisted, canines were paddling about everywhere, yipping their compatriots to vacate dog-clogged banks and shores, barking them inland. The bases of Delta willows and cottonwoods shone egg-yolk yellow, and the bottoms of Valley oaks soon became moist blond as the horde of dogs spread out to populate California.

Some of the felines fortunate enough to have smacked land upright snacked on the carnage of dead field mice trampled in the canine stampede. Others climbed the stained trees, swallowing unsuspecting birds.

Cats who had not smacked land (upright, downright, or sideways) made a mess of Winslow's afternoon. Islands of decomposing cat corpses rose from the slough at low tide. The water became putrefied, dispatching Winslow and the other inhabitants—the crawdads, the clams, the mud and grass shrimps—to the clear flow of the nearby River.

The famous *homo sapien* scientist Charles Darwin had completed a long day of stuffing critters into bottles of formaldehyde, pinning bugs onto cork board, and chopping up various amphibians in a frenzy of anatomical inquisitiveness. He leaned on the gunnel of the anchored *H.M.S. Beagle* and stared across the Galapagos bay, a thousand pairs of beady giant lizard eyes staring back. "I've got it! I'll call it *evolution*!" he yelled over to the lizards.

God heard Darwin's word echo off the Galapagos rocks. "Evolution? What the heck, someone should give it a try," God said to no one in particular.

Mother Nature hear God's words echo off the cosmos and took the hint. "Mutate, grow, adapt, replicate," she commanded the strands of DNA floating in the putrid pile of rapidly decomposing protein in Snodgrass Slough.

When Winslow returned sometime later, Snodgrass Slough was again clear and clean, and alive with his previous neighbors the clams, crawdads, and shrimps. Plus a bunch of new piscine critters who soon taught him to play games of catch-the-clam, tag-you're-it, and Marco Polo in the eddies and backwaters on lazy Delta days.

"Meow," they said to Winslow.

S A L L Y ' S M E N

"Ten tHousand River CommisSions, with
the mineS of the woRld at their back,
cannot taMe that laWless s t r e a m ,
cannot cURb it or confine it, c a n n o t say
to it "Go Here' or "Go There',and
make it oBey; cannOt s a v e a shoRe
which it has sentenCed; cannot bAr its path
with an obstrUction which it will
nOT tear down, dance over and laugH at.
But a discreTe man will not put
these thinGs into sPoken wOrds."

Mark Twain, *Life of the Mississippi* (courtesy of Jeff Mount).

*G*enerally speaking, the men in my mom's life have been nothing but trouble. Her grand-daddy Ossian, the famous story teller, was a notable exception. He died in 1950 when she was either seven or eight. I never got a chance to know him.

I have brothers and half-brothers living throughout the Delta of central California. Sisters and half-sisters too. The first were born when Mom was twenty five; others followed like clockwork eight years apart. Some of the kids were sired in the same place, on the same day, as half siblings. Others—born eight (or sixteen, or twenty four)—years apart are full sisters and brothers. This makes my family tree confusing.

I witnessed the second to last procreation. It was held at Steamboat Slough—across the levee road from where Marty the Artist, Sherry, and Winslow (he's their kid) live in a two story, renovated white farm house with a lone but stately palm tree in front. Mom dropped hundreds of eggs while the potential pops—there were five in all—squirted sperms by the millions beside her. Sixteen days later when the eggs hatched, scores of millimeter-tall half-Sallys hovered the bottom. Within a week, there were maybe two dozen of my brothers and sisters left uneaten by our neighbors (the crawdads, clams and catfish) or by the herd of striped bass which had happened by, headed upriver on their own reproductive expedition. That was eight years ago. Now there are just two: Delores and Dirk.

Sally—that's my mom's name—bred again just a few months back, breaking with white sturgeon tradition by doing it near the headwater of the Feather River, up where the green sturgeon live. A *sapien* named Carpenter accompanied her; you may have heard about it. It caused quite a hullabaloo.

Mom made me stay home to keep an eye on my little brother and sister; there's no telling what kind of trouble a pair of eight years-olds could get into, left unattended. I was glad, actually. I'm a little shy and, though Mom doesn't know it, still kinda scared of The River. And Carpenter makes me nervous. When he's with Mom, it's like having a step-dad around. You know what I mean?

Arlene and Aretha, my two surviving sisters from Mom's first time, moved over to Snodgrass Slough with their kids last week. It was getting crowded at Steamboat, what with the two Ds and me (I'm a B, the only one left of the second laying) living at home. Plus there's now a tribe of Es who made it downriver from the adventure up in the Feather that I mentioned. Soon there will be less. I hope at least a couple make it to the naming time, which we traditionally hold on their first birthday. Mom said I get to pick them. I'm considering Ernie, Ellie, East and Elaine. We'll see.

Arlie is another matter. He swam off to San Francisco Bay over twenty years ago, yet gossip of his deeds still floats back up every so often. Too often, if you ask me, because it inevitably gets Mom all upset.

Just the other day an old sturge came by and bubbled out a rumor. "Heard first fin from a fella who lives off Alcatraz that Arlie was up to some shenanigans again," the sturge told Mom.

"I'm happy to hear he's still alive," Mom replied.

"That boy's nothin' but trouble, Ms. Sally. He's nothin' like the rest of your clan. His pa must have been a mean one."

"Well, his two sisters sure turned out sweet," I blurted back at the old codger. "I'll bet Aretha and Arlene had the same father, and I'll bet ya he was no father to Arlie, I'll bet ya that," I said, surprising myself. I'm usually timid around strangers.

"No bets from me, miss. Arlie's so mean you'd think his pa was a son of Bentley," he said, referring to Ossian's famous fish tale of the contemptuous and gargantuan sturgeon of olde who over-gorged on ghost shrimps and got so fat he got stuck in a bend in Miner Slough and sunk, becoming the ballast of a small island still there today.

Mom couldn't stand it. "How do *you* know Arlie's so mean, old fish? Have you ever even met my son? I'm sick and tired of you Bay sturgeon coming up here just to spread vicious lies about my boy. Who gave you the right to criticize my boy?"

"Well pardon *me,* Ms. Sally Sturgeon. Just pardon me," said the visitor, stirring up the silt, further clouding the already murky Sacramento. "You know, you've been nothin' but uppity and high nosed ever since you met that *sapien* Carpet Man who can listen and talk sturgeonese. He and you going up the Feather—why, that was disgusting! I'm tellin' you, Ms. Sally: you're getting a reputation as nothin' but a high fallootin' *sapien* lover. And I'll tell you somethin' else: fishes from Suisun Bay to the Golden Gate are sayin' your boy Arlie ain't nothing but a white trash sturgeon, and a killer to boot."

"The sapien's name is Carpenter, . . . and a killer? Now you're calling my little boy . . . a *killer*?" Mom exhaled, sending such a stream of bubbles to the surface that had Marty the Artist been on his front porch, he would have heard the word *killer* echo from levee to levee. He probably wasn't, and he can't hear sturgeon anyway, but I'm telling you: Mom was pissed.

"Said it. Meant it. About time you heard it," replied the visitor.

"Get out of my slough, you gizzardless old kelp sucker. Get yourself back to the Bay. I hope to Posideon you get snagged on a ghost shrimp lined to a *sapien* on the way. You and your vicious, slandering clan. You make me sick. Get out of here now."

With that, the old sturge turned snout to tail and retreated in a huff downstream.

See what I mean? Nothing but trouble.

Mom and I swam upriver to Carpenter's place the next morning. He lives on the east bank of the Sacramento between Bryte Bend and the Taylor Monument in a rambling wood and brick house which he shares with Janie, his wife, and which was shared briefly, the year before their arrival, with the Sacramento itself. The River moved in for a week in the spring of '86, leaving its mark on cabinets and baseboards. *Sapien* visitors are impressed with this reminder of who really owns the property.

When we arrived, Carpenter was on the dock repairing the altimeter for his pontoon boat. I've never understood the utility of an altimeter for river life, but the ways of *sapiens* are often strange to me, so I've never brought it up with Mom. She is very accepting of Carpenter's views and habits, rarely scolding him for drinking so much beer and smoking too many cigarettes, creating tall tales of The River, and abiding friends who slaughter *us* with line and pole. She'd never let any of us kids do any of those things.

For whatever reason, Mom and he get along real well. One time she happened by there when he was doing his Wednesday morning River report, live—through the telephone—for a local radio station. It was March and he was actually standing in The River which had flooded his entire backyard. As he reported on the essential River conditions—like the temperature, the humidity, and the fact that it was flowing downstream—Mom snuck up and nibbled his toes. I don't know much about this radio and telephone stuff, but when Mom tells the story, it is pretty funny.

She fins up to visit and chat with him nearly every Sunday. How she obtained this oral talent is less mysterious to me than the altimeter gadget on the boat, or the radiophonic stuff, or Carpenter's friend Alex who hands out free ghost shrimps to all the sturgeon of the Delta. Mom's gift is explained in "The Tornado," we sturgeon's account of the creation of the animals who live <u>above</u> water. It is a long story—chronicled by *Somesturgeon*—involving Mische Nahma, queen of the fishes, and how she tricked old Neptune, king of the sea, into letting some of the ancient fish become amphibians, reptiles, birds, and mammals.

Somesturgeon gave me the gift of seeing above water. No one else in the family has it, except, of course, Mom. I'm actually a little embarrassed about it. I don't like the responsibility. Sometimes I wish I was one of my half-sisters instead of myself.

Somesturgeon gave Mom the additional gift of talking above water. To the land animals called *sapiens,* Mom is a very, very special sturgeon.

When we rose from the bottom of The River to the edge of the dock, Mom gave a wag of her tail to catch Carpenter's attention. She soaked him. "That you Sally Sturgeon?" he yelled, without even looking. Most *sapiens* assume that Carpenter gave her that name. He didn't. She had it way before they met. Everyone in The River, the Delta and the bays beyond knows her as Sally Sturgeon, like they all know her grand-daddy, the teller of fish tales, by the name Ossian. I'm from a famous sturgeon family.

"Morning Carpenter," she said.

"Good ride up here?"

"Piece of kelp. Tides were right. And The River, she be low and slow. Brought my daughter of the second brood along with me. She's the shy one; name is B. You've met?"

"Oh sure," he said. "Good morning to you, Miss B."

Morning to you, Mister Carpenter, I thought (since, of course, I couldn't speak to the *sapien*).

"Glad you came up with your mom," he continued, knowing not to expect a response to his salutation. "Haven't seen you since the egging party that Winslow and his parents threw for Sally down on Steamboat Slough just before she got laid the last time. The time up on the Feather. Been nearly six months, I figure."

She didn't get *laid,* I thought. Fish don't date before they mate; they don't fall in love and get laid, for Poseidon's sake! The girls plop eggs and the boys squirt sperm and that's that. All this *sapien* anthropomorphism is silly. If Carpenter hangs around with Mom too long, he might start believing that owls are wise, lions are noble, and beluga whales have feelings.

"I need the bottom of the old pontoon boat scraped clean," he said. "Any chance you gals could flip on your backs and suck off all the algae and guck that's under there?"

Guck sucking? I thought.

"If you'll do me a favor in return," Mom said.

"What's that, Sally?"

"I need to find Arlie."

"The kid from your first brood who ran away?"

"That's the one. I've heard he's causing more trouble. Maybe just fishy rumors, but I thought that if we could find him. . . and maybe I could talk with him. . . well, maybe he'd want to come home to Steamboat and settle down for a while. . ."

"You OK, Sally?"

"Oh Carpenter, I'm so tired of hearing all these stories about my boy. I want my boy to come home," Mom said to him. I'd never heard her so remorseful. Water welled in my eyes.

"What kind of trouble this time, Sally?"

"An old sturge from the Bay claims he killed someone."

"Another sturgeon?"

"Nothing else would matter."

"Killed his own kind?"

"Arlie's been blamed for lots of things, but I can't believe this one's true. I don't deny that he's a tough kid. But I can't believe he'd kill another of us. Will you help me, Carpenter?"

"You know I will," the *sapien* said. "We can start looking for Arlie tomorrow. You'll be joining us, B?"

I'd never been on one of Mom and Carpenter's adventures. It's my preference to stay near home where it's safe. But being invited by the infamous *sapien* was quite an honor, and I didn't want to embarrass Mom by declining. So I raised my tail in the affirmative.

Carpenter claimed that though the pontoon boat was a veteran of many peregrinations upon The River, it required some special outfitting for an extended trip down to The Bay. An excuse for upgrading his boat with new gadgets and gizmos, he'd admitted when Mom pressed him. "Boys and their toys," Mom once overheard Janie explain it.

We cleaned the bottom while he was gone shopping. Algae and other lower life forms are not my favorite food, though I don't mind them. Mom found a few freshwater barnacles buried in the guck; they are a treat, and she shared them as you would expect.

Carpenter returned from the boat gadget store, bumping a wheelbarrow full of stuff down the cleated ramp to the dock. Electronical stuff that I can't pronounce and haven't a clue as to what it might be good for. I asked my mom to ask the *sapien* about it.

"Hey Carpenter, what's all that stuff for?"

"It's the latest in high-tech boating stuff, Sally. I'm trying to catch up with all the devices you sturgeon own."

"We don't own anything," said my mom.

"Do to," said Carpenter. "You have senses that work like bottom finders and depth gauges and current indicators and salinity measurers and speedometers and compasses. All built in at birth, courtesy of 200 million years of work by none other than Mother Nature herself. I just shelled out nearly four grand, and you're still three senses ahead of me."

He then rattled off the list of the stuff to my mom, who wasn't really listening. He didn't seem to care. Judging from the smile on his face, I think he enjoys just hearing the sounds of the words for his toys.

Carpenter set to his work installing all the stuff alongside the altimeter, pausing occasionally for a beer and a smoke, or a chat with my mom. I finned around the neighborhood, trading shrimp stories with some local cats, and had a nice clam lunch with Mom on the bottom. Towards sunset, the pontoon boat was ready.

"You want to spend the night here?" he asked.

"Sure. Why not?" Mom said. "We can head downriver together in the morning. But we need to stop at my place on Steamboat Slough to lock up the house, take out the garbage, feed the cats and leave a note for the neighbors saying we might be gone for a few weeks."

My mom has been hanging around this *sapien* too long. Take out the garbage indeed!

Burble, burble, burble. The sound of a boat motor snapped me from a sound sleep. Props and rudders and keels scare me so much that the gravel in my gizzard rattles at the sound or sight of them.

I went up top to see what time it was. The sky was that faint gray just ahead of dawn. The deck of the pontoon boat was illuminated with red and green running lights, and the bright white of a sputtering Coleman lantern hung from the six foot chunk of bent aluminum conduit that Carpenter claims as a mast.

"Top of the morning, Miss B," he said.

I waved my dorsal in recognition.

"It's time to head out. Sally up yet?"

Good question. I dove back to the bottom, expecting her to still be snoozing under the cottonwood sinker where we'd spent the night, but she wasn't there. Figuring I'd missed her going up while I was coming down, I rose again.

"Hey B, let's get a move on! Go wake up that sleepy-head mom of yours. I'll bet you a dozen crawdad tails sautéed in garlic and butter that I can beat you two downriver! Me and the pontoon boat against you two; we'll race you from here to the turnoff at Steamboat. How 'bout it?"

I dove once again and searched the bottom far and wide. Three green sturgeon drifted by. Hesitantly, I asked if they had seen my mom. I wasn't surprised when there was no reply; the greens are an odd breed—you never know what they are thinking, what they're up to. The channel catfish that live under Carpenter's dock were just waking up. Seen Sally? No ma'am, they said. I would have continued interrogating the local aquatic critters, but all that remained were crawdads, clams and tube worms. None of them can talk. I'm not sure that clams even know how to think.

Hummmm. This *is* very odd. I surfaced for the third time and the dawn had burst full. Carpenter had shut down the Coleman and the running lights, and was pacing the sixteen by eight foot plywood pontoon boat deck. He beckoned me over.

"Any luck?"

I didn't move a fin or a barbel. He took this to mean *no,* and said: "Maybe she decided to go ahead without us. Miss B, you head downstream. Fin-and-tail your little heart out; see if you can catch her. I'll fire up the Yamaha and meet you across from Marty the Artist's place."

Something was *wrong*. My mom hadn't *ever* left me without at least a tail-wave of good-bye. But there was nothing else to do but head down to Steamboat Slough, and fast.
I went to the bottom, inhaled two crawdads who weren't paying attention, and put my appendages into overdrive.

I got there before him, wondering if the bet was still on. As a matter of necessity, sturgeon eat crawdads alive and whole: claws to tail, including the orangey-green gooey stuff inside their upper cavity and head—the whole shebang. But Carpenter's recipe for tails-only is so delicious, why I'd swim a league to get just one.

Carpenter comes down to Steamboat Slough every Christmas. On Christmas morning, all the kids—me, Arlene, Aretha, any Cs that are visiting, and Delores and Dirk—fetch craw-dads from the slough bottom with our famous vacuum cleaner mouths. We hold the dads by the tail trying not to swallow them into our gizzards (which is tricky since we don't have teeth), and then spit them onto the bank at Carpenter's feet. When the pile gets big enough, he goes up the levee and over to Marty the Artist's house and cooks up a big garlicky, buttery batch, and splits it between us kids and any *sapiens* who are hanging around. As you can imagine, the pile on the bank has to be pretty big. A lot of work, but worth every tail of it.

I got there before him, nervous. I looked for Mom in the usual places. I tried waiting on the bottom, hoping she'd swum off to tell a neighbor of our impending journey in search of Arlie.

I got there before him and I was alone. The D twins were with Aretha and Arlene, up at their new place in Snodgrass Slough. I had no one to talk to. True, there were still Es around (though less than when I'd left), but talking was months away for them. I hugged the bottom and cried.

My mom had disappeared.

I heard the drone of a boat motor followed by the glubble-glubble of an anchor flying to the bottom. Must be Carpenter. I finned the tears away and rose.

The look on his face told me he knew. He asked, quietly: "Sally?"

I was shaking. That told him the answer. He dropped into one of the weather-beaten captain's chairs and stared at the water. "You stay here, B. I'm going up to Marty the Artist's place. He'll know what to do."

I spent a restless night at the bottom of a back eddy in one of my mom's favorite sleeping holes. I had horrible, piscine dreams. Of giant squid with beaks the size of Carpenter's pontoon boat who tortured young sturgeon by popping huge suction cups up and down their bodies, loosening the cartilaginous plates and distending their barbels. Of a fire spitting flying animal whose quest for ocean run green sturgeon rivaled the tale of Ahab and the great white whale. Of endless, repeating stanzas of Longfellow's poem of the death of Mische Nahma at the hands of Hiawatha on the shores of Gitche Gumee. And of my best friend Fellicia who was chopped in two by the propeller of a giant cargo ship near Carquinez Strait—she shouldn't have gone down there, I told her *not to go* down there.

"You OK, B?" Carpenter asked when he returned in the morning.

I floated, motionless.

"Marty the Artist and I talked the missing-Sally situation over. First we thought she could have had a gizzard blockage or an air bladder failure or a fin seizure, and just drowned. But you would have seen her, right?"

I nodded. I've seen many a dead fish suspended underwater before they bloat with decay and rise to the surface on their way to heaven.

"Then we thought maybe she simply got a burr under her fin about something—like me asking her to guck-suck the pontoon bottoms—and took off upstream in a huff; you know how independent she can be. But she would've said something to you, at least said good-bye, right?"

I nodded. Mom never left me without finning a good-bye.

"Well, this morning I was rummaging the refrigerator for a beer while Sherry was helping Winslow eat his oatmeal, and the little fella looked up from his bowl and said: 'Sally's gone 'cause stolen.' The more Marty the Artist and Sherry and I talked it through, the more Sherry convinced me that her kid was right. Women's intuition and all that."

I nodded. Even though I'm young, I've had an intuition now and again myself.

"So, B, here it is: we think that your mom has been kidnapped. By a gang of green sturgeon set on revenge. Revenge for me and your mom's meddling in their home turf. Revenge for her getting laid there in their Feather's headwaters. I feel terrible; I should *never* have agreed to let her go up there."

Kidnapped? I was pretty sure that kidnap was different than kill. Kidnap is not a word sturgeon find much use for. I decided *kidnapped* meant Mom might still be alive.

"We think the greens are holding her hostage, demanding a ransom from you whites."

Hostage and ransom. Holy carp, more strange words!

"If we're right, the greens will let the word out to every white sturgeon from here to the Golden Gate. That's where you come in, B. You know that Sally is the only sturgeon I can hear. It will be your job to keep your ears to the bottom and find out where they've got her. Can you do it?"

Did I have a choice? I raised my tail *yes*.

Carpenter told me to meet him at the east end of Snag Island, just past Honker Bay, just in case we got separated on the way down. Not a chance. I stayed with that pontoon boat like a barnacle on a piling, being careful, of course, to avoid the propeller.

I'd never swam above the bottom for any distance to smell of. I'll confess that it was exciting, finning and tailing under the double bow wakes, ducking the floating debris. Keeping up was no sweat; even at full throttle, his little Yamaha pushed the floating platform no faster than ten knots. Plus we were going downhill.

If I lost sight of him (which could easily happen), I could still hear him. And if that sense failed, I still had my best one in reserve: smell. I could smell Carpenter and his craft a league away, maybe two.

Carpenter cut the engine as we approached Snag Island, let the current and the outgoing tide drift him toward shore, and tossed the anchor in twenty feet of water. I was on top of it and by his side before he'd popped another beer. His fifth since leaving Steamboat. I'd heard each one. "Nice run down here, hey B? Too bad it wasn't a pleasure cruise; I'd've enjoyed it a lot more. We're going to spend the night here, if it's OK with you."

I liked the plural. Last night was the first I'd ever spent alone anywhere, and that was back at home. Being alone in a bay of some foreign island made me real nervous, so I quickly raised my tail *yes*.

"I've got salami and French bread for dinner. Want some?"

I flipped my tail sideways *no*. Though I'd heard those food words before, I had no idea what they actually were. Carpenter's famous sautéed tails were the only non-sturgeon food I'd ever inhaled.

But I was hungry. I hadn't eaten anything since the double-dad snack back at Carpenter's dock the morning before. If I went searching for food, losing sight of his boat was a given. With the engine off, I wouldn't be able to hear him (unless he extended his beer streak). It was time for a test of the old schnazolla. I'd have to smell for dinner and smell for Carpenter at the same time. Oh buoy!

I dove straight down and sniffed about, probing the muck and silt. A big Dungeness crab—too big for my gizzard—and lots of *sapien* detritus. I headed away from the boat, cautiously. Two ghost shrimps and a green olive. Oh, oh. Luckily, I'd heard about this *sapien* trick from Mom. Shades of old Alex and his invisible ghost shrimps-on-a-hook scam! The *sapien* at the other end of this line had taken the bait literally, attaching real ghost shrimps to the hook instead of the invisible, non-existent ones sold by Keith Fraser, the famous *sapien* sturgeon guru. I nudged the ensemble with my snout just to give the fisherman a thrill. Varoom went the bait across the bottom as he yanked it hard. Hey, this is fun!

I nosed around the bottom some more, this time catching the scent of something delectable. My barbels flickered. My brain connected the smell and the touch to my protruding proboscis mouth—and I inhaled, hard. Bingo! Mud shrimps. A whole bevy of mud shrimps. I sucked them off the bottom until my tummy bulged.

Inflating my swim bladder against the mass of shrimps, I went topside beneath a dark and foggy night. Carpenter was reading, and sipping, under the glow of the hissing Coleman. I splashed my tail. He waved his hand. I went down to a night's sleep, hopefully free of Hiawathan, Mische Nahmaish, Gitche Gumeed nightmares.

The sky broke orange as I broke the surface less than a hundred yards from the boat. The incoming tide and the outgoing current had unwittingly conspired to maintain me at bay. Carpenter was stooped over the Coleman lantern's brother, frying the unborn young of a land-air creature and slabs of smoked porcine in an aluminum pan.

"Eggs, B?"

No, I tailed. Then it hit me: what if the kidnappers had stolen Mom upstream? Maybe we were heading down the wrong watery trail, following The River toward its ultimate end beyond the exit beneath the Golden Arches—into what we sturgeon call the Big Water. What if instead they had taken her back to the pool on the Feather near the fish hatchery where the Es had been conceived? Or another tributary of The River: the Yuba, the American, the Bear? Or even some feeder of The River's San Joaquin sister, like the Mokelumne, the Merced, the Cosumnes?

"Bacon?"

Maybe they are even more devious than the Marty the Artist family imagined, and they had pried open the fish screen at Clifton Court Forebay and entered the California Aqueduct and were heading for Los Angeles while Carpenter ate his scrambled eggs. El A! My mother is being canalled to La La Land.

"Toast with kumquat jelly?"

Worse: the hoodlums have taken my mama to the Salton Sea, drugged on low doses of the piscicide rotenone. No, to Hoover Dam; she's shackled to an intake pipe five hundred feet above the whirring turbines. No, they've already sold her into slavery at Sea World in San Diego; she'll spend the remaining fifty years of her life confined to a tank, fed artificial fish food pellets made of sardines entrails and moldy soybean meal.

"Cold beer?"

That stopped me cold in my paranoiac tracks. Actually made me laugh. I'd no more drink liquid from a can than he would drink water from The River. Carpenter was a major adherent to the W.C. Fields school of liquidity—*water?. . . never touch the stuff . . . fish fuck in it.* The spell broken, I raised my head and stared straight at him, hoping he had a plan, wishing he would share it.

"Here's our plan, B," he said, after less than a minute of me staring.

Wasn't that interesting? I might try the wishing and staring combination again, I thought.

Carpenter continued: "The tide's turned and is riding the back of the current. That means there should be lots of your fellow whites feeding in San Pablo Bay. We'll drift down there, sorta la-de-da like. You'll go to work on the bottom, listening. I'll hail the fishing boats and ask the captains and mates whether there's been a sudden glut of greens about. You with me?"

Tail rise.

"Sure you don't want some breakfast?"

Tail waggle.

"Nothing like bacon, beer and eggs to start a morning on the water," he said, followed by a belch. "It's the most important meal of the day, you know."

I was thinking about interrogating the first green sturgeon of the day, not sucking the first beer. As I practiced my lines, my anger grew. Excuse me, oh great inhabitant of the upper River—seen a white named Sally Sturgeon hereabouts? Pardon me Mister Green— heard anything about a white ransom? Hey green; yeah, you, over there—are you one of the slimy kidnappers? Look buddy; tell me everything you know about Sally Sturgeon or I'll kill you and every last one of your kelp sucking, mother stealing kind.

I was becoming like Arlie.

We had three choices for getting to San Pablo Bay from Snag Island. Rather, Carpenter's pontoon boat had three; mine were only a few short of infinite. Actual islands posed limitations to us both, but as long as there was a foot or more of something mostly aqueous, I could fin anywhere.

The pontoon boat elected not to take a small detour northwest past Freeman Island, head through the Suisun Cutoff (no shallower than thirty feet at "mean lower low water" according to Carpenter's NOAA Nautical Chart No. 18652), turn south at Grizzly Bay into Suisun Bay, and then aim for the old C&H sugar refinery perched on the shore of the Strait of Carquinez.

The pontoon boat also elected not to detour south (fifteen feet were guaranteed), catch the main ship channel which runs straight west into Suisun Bay, and then aim for the Interstate-80 steel *sapien* bridge twins perched high above the Strait of Carquinez.

The pontoon boat, instead, chose to aim straight *at* Suisun Bay, through the shallows called Middle Ground (the reason for the naming eluding Carpenter, temporarily) which it

struck (the proverbial light bulb going off in Carpenter's head shortly thereafter) at a tide·
just a tad lower than the "mean lower low" of two feet noted on the aforementioned chart.
It was so shallow that my pelvic and anal fins left grooves in the mud as I pushed my way to
the side of the now immobile craft.

"Shit," he said.

Inattention to electronical gadgets? I wondered.

"Why didn't you warn me?" he shouted. "Sally always took care of the underwater details
of boating for me," he yelled. "This would never have happened if I'd had a *competent*
sturgeon as first mate," he screamed.

Same to you, you nautical device loving *sapien*. Plug in the dam depth finder and read
the dam charts next time. The animate members of the rescue team were becoming edgy;
the third had become stuck.

Tides fall. Tides rise. Carpenter awaited the later, reading a book of Delta history out-loud,
sipping on the ever-present beer. Around beer three, the once-shiny aluminum bottom was
released by the muck. Carpenter pushed the pontoon boat toward deeper water using the
pipe that claimed fame as the mast and which held the single 12 volt bulb that warned other
craft—like rugby field sized oil tankers—of his presence in the night. When the propeller of
the outboard was free, he fired up the Yamaha and we were on our way.

I met the first sturgeon—a big white—about forty feet down, opposite the Naval Weapons
Station on the outskirts of Port Chicago. Carpenter had just read out loud that there was
once a town named The City of New York of the Pacific, founded in 1849 by a Colonel
Stevenson (of the New York Volunteers) and a Dr. W. C. Parker. In the early 1900s the town
was renamed Pittsburg, after its sister in Pennsylvania, though the sister spells herself with
a final *h*. The cadence of *City of New York of the Pacific* reminded me of *Sally of Steamboat
Slough of the Delta*. I asked the sturge whether she'd been seen or heard of.

"Yep," it said.

"Yep, what? Heard or seen?"

"Heard. Everybody's heard of Sally. She's the famous grand-daughter of old Ossian, the
famous teller of fish tales."

"Have you seen her?"

"Nope."

"Have you seen any suspicious greens hereabouts?"

"Well son. . . or is it miss? Which are you?" it asked, since, as you know, you can't tell a sturgeon's sex from its outside.

"Miss B's my name."

"Well Miss B, all them greens look suspicious to me. Don't trust 'em farther than I can see 'em," he said, which, as you know, meant he didn't trust them at *all* given the sturgeon's notoriously poor eyesight.

"Did hear some talk though," he continued. "A school of halibut yacking about some commotion at a place downcurrent from here. An island. Begins with *are.*"

"Ryer Island?"

"No ma'am. Wasn't that. Can't recall it. *Rrr* somethin'."

"Thanks anyways," I said to it. I was anxious to find Carpenter before the pontoon boat drifted too far away, so I headed up.

There he was, a hundred yards off, tied alongside a party boat named *Slough Sisters*, talking with the captain. There were customers aboard, lines taut against the tide. When one started yelling and pointing toward me, I took a dive and finned over to safety beneath the pontoon boat.

Mom had once explained that Carpenter couldn't protect us from the habits of the fishermen, not directly. Like, he couldn't tell another *sapien:* "Don't catch <u>that</u> one. Her name's Sally Sturgeon, she's my good friend." When I asked her why, she shrugged her pectorals and said something about how special *sapiens* like Carpenter have to keep their relationship with fish a secret from the other *sapiens*. Otherwise, the other *sapiens* would confiscate his pontoon boat and make him move far away. Mom said the other *sapiens* would make him live in a bad place with padded walls, a place up on the land that we could never visit.

I don't know much about walls and land, and even less about air. We are taught some things about these non-aqueous places through the wise words of *Somesturgeon,* the ancient fish who recorded "The Tornado" legend, way back in piscine antiquity. I can't ask Carpenter about the bad lands or why he can't tell other *sapiens* about me, because I can't talk to him. I can only listen. Only my mom can talk to Carpenter; my mom is a very special fish.

But she's also a very special mom. And right now I don't have a mom and nobody has seen her. And right now I wish Carpenter would stop talking to the *sapiens* on the big fish-slaughtering boat and start looking for my mom instead.

The putt, putt, putt of the Yamaha finally commenced. I stayed a few feet down, right between the two pontoons, as we headed downcurrent. When the motor stopped, I figured it was safe again. Carpenter was leaning over the railing waiting for me when I came up.

"Anyone seen your mom?" he asked.

I waggled my tail *no*.

"Any word about her at all?" he asked.

I raised my tail up and waggled it sideways at the same time, trying to indicate *sort of* to him. It didn't work. This communicating in *yes-no* binary code was a pain in the tail. If we continued at this game of "ten questions," we wouldn't find my mom until the next century.

I tried to figure a way to use the game of charades. You know: looks like? smells like? feels like? Arlene and Aretha and their kids and I used to spend long, tule-fogged winter days in Steamboat Slough doing piscine charades. But the game was of no use here, adrift with this *sapien* in the lower reaches of The River. I was motherless and equipped with nothing but a stupid yes-no, zero-one, on-off tail. Carpenter might as well be asking questions of his pontoon boat.

I tried to think of a way to tell him the word *island*. An island that began with the sound *rrr*. I closed my tiny, beady, nearly useless eyes and thought hard: AR ISLAND. I tucked in my four barbels so I wouldn't be distracted by the feel of the water or any passing debris. I let 200 million years of *Acipenser transmontanus* past buried in my 240 chromosomes twist and turn ISLAND RRR-something around, hoping for a clever trick to make Carpenter understand we had to go there. I shut down my most important sense—the one that could detect a hatch of herring roe five miles away—and thought: ARE as in roe, ISLAND as in island, RRRR, ISLAND, ARE, ISLAND, R ISLAND. . .

"Maybe Sally's over by Roe Island," Carpenter whooped. I snapped out of my meditation and flipped my tail three times. Was it a coincidence? Carpenter can't hear me because I can't talk *sapien,* but can he <u>think</u> me? Maybe I can <u>think</u> at him!

I tried it again. Close the eyes; fold up the feelers; shut down the sniffer; concentrate: COLD BEER.

The familiar *pop* of an aluminum tab echoed off the water.

"Don't mind if I do," said Carpenter. "Thanks for reminding me."

Well I'll be beached and by gollied! I think I can actually *think* him! I decided to give it one more try, just to be sure. I MISS MOM.

"I miss your mom too, Miss B," said Carpenter. "Let's head down to Roe Island and see if she's there. It's only a few miles further, just this side of the Carquinez Straits."

Holy Carp, it works! I can think a *sapien*. I *am* special! I may not be able to talk to Carpenter like her, but I can *think* at him! I can't wait to tell Mom about this. If we can find her. If she's alive. If the evil greens haven't killed her. Carpenter, LET'S GO.

"We're on our way, Miss B," he yelled over the varoom of the Yamaha starting up. "Roe Island is *dead* ahead."

Carpenter certainly had a way with words. The men in my mom's life—aren't they something?

Carpenter's book on the history of the Delta doesn't have an entry for Roe Island. However, even a fish of little brain could take a good guess at the origin of the name.

The island is now uninhabited. The shores long washed clean of the bony plates and cartilage remains of the decomposed bodies from the carnage of egg hunting a hundred years ago, back when most white sturgeon lived to be a hundred years or more, many reaching a half ton. Before the slaughters, the sturgeon slaughters. Male and female, young and old, by the thousands—snared with gill nets and hooked on steel lines. The young ones were discarded dead or dying from the fishermen's boats, hundreds of pounds too light for the trouble. The old ones, too big to haul aboard, were gaffed or roped aside the killing crafts and dragged alive but drowning—their gills high in the poisonous air—through the shallows of Suisun Bay or from the deep channel at Carquinez Strait to the little island with a flat sandy beach, pleasant to see on a fogless bay day. Winched up on the shore, lined in a row or stacked like pulpwood. Flinching and flickering, tails cut to drain the blood away from the egg sacks, should they prove to be females, later, when the knife tore open the belly from anus to mouth. Or just dying a slow male death, blood dripping from the incision, bony plates desiccating in the hot sun, brain chanting ancient mantras of *Somesturgeon* legends, awaiting the pointless, eggless death on the land. Pointless death on the land.

Carpenter cut the engine a hundred yards from the south shore, letting the current drift the pontoon boat silently past. I rose to its side.

"There's little for me to do now, Miss B," he said. "It's pretty much up to you. Be careful. If you see a herd of greens, high-tail it out of there and come find me. I'll be anchored a half-mile down, just above the C&H Sugar Refinery at Crockett. And, please, be very careful. You're the only sturgeon friend I've got!"

There he goes again—attempting levity like a typical, insensitive male. Talking like Mom is already dead. Turned out later that his anchoring was a big mistake, but I agreed with him on the being careful part. It's true I'd gained some self-confidence these past few days (plus my new ability to *think* him), but I was still a bashful and cautious twenty year old slough-girl from the quiet sidewaters of the Sacramento River—and, tell you the truth, I was scared to death.

I shot Carpenter a THANKS, acknowledged his wave good-bye with a slap of my tail, and watched him motor away. Alone again.

I dropped down a few feet and took a deep snort. Off to my right was the smell of something piscine, too far away to identify specie-wise. I closed my eyes—why bother—and flexed my barbels. Down another ten feet, I finned and tailed steadily through the current toward the island. The tide was near slack. The water was the murky chocolate brown that we sturgeon so favor. A school of freshmen striped bass swam past me, heading up to the Delta for their first feel of freshwater since they descended post-birth. Down the last five feet to the bottom. I grazed a big halibut half-buried in the silt, excusing myself in a whisper, adding: "Have you seen a white, about twice my size, goes by the name of Sally?" The halibut motioned its topside eyes to the right. I aimed that way and smelled deeply. Rusted iron and rotted wood.

I'd caught that same smell many a time back up in The River. The smell of an intact sailing ship lying sideways and silent on the bottom from a moonless night collision with a cotton-wood sinker or planter. The thousand shards of a once mighty paddle wheeler ripped by the explosion of the boiler, a drunken engineer's neglect. A barge once piled a hundred tons high with sacks of wheat harvested from the plains of the Montezuma Hills, scuttled by a farmer in competition for a penny a pound profit. Or scows run aground, houseboats beached and abandoned, cabin cruisers burned to the waterline from all manner of sapien neglect and confusion.

Rotted wood and rusted iron. And green.

The halibut suddenly drew up from the mud and flapped away. I leaned to the left and smelled green, lots of green, approaching. I spun head to tail, and there was green there too. I was surrounded. I emptied my swim bladder like a WWII submarine cracked open from a depth-charge attack, escaping the sure death of deep water for a chance of survival on the surface, no where to go but up. It was to no avail. They were above me too, a dozen or more, slimy green, ugly and scowling. I was had.

And they had Carpenter too. He was being towed by his anchor chain by two of the biggest thresher sharks I'd ever smelled, his valiant 30-horse Yamaha no match for the ancient fish now in cahoots with the Green villains from the Feather River.

I was herded into the decomposed stern of the sunken ship, guarded by three greens and two tigers. Sharks—the lowest form of the piscine world, despised by all others for their stupidity and ruthlessness. The only ancients, other than the paddlefish and we sturgeon, to survive from the Jurrasic. Two hundred million years of swimming the seas, and they had advanced by less than a finfull of chromosomes. They had been egged on, I suspected, by the evil *Acipenser medirostris* greens with some promise of retribution against we *Acipenser transmontanus* whites.

I was sure that my mom was here also, though the decay of the prison and the stench of the sharks blocked any scent of her.

I could hear Carpenter above us, marooned on the deck of his pontoon boat, screaming obscenities at the invisible perpetrators. He was in no imminent danger if he stayed put—though he was surely facing the horror of a rapidly declining beer supply.

That was his problem. I had another: the arrival at the entrance of my prison cell of a green sturgeon so big that I could actually see it. It turned out to be a she, name of Gloria. Gloria Green, bitch queen of the Feather River clan. Sister to Glorenda who was married (greens are different from us whites in more ways than color and disposition) to a guy who lived under the dock of Frank Kaiser's Lochness Bait Shop at San Rafael. Past tense. Died last year in a fight with a white.

Arlie.

I awoke before dawn remembering Gloria's words to me the night before. "Darlin'," she'd said, "you're going to get to see your white trash mama real soon. Real soon. . . just before you die. Together. Slow like. Sweet dreams, darlin'."

So Carpenter's theory, based on his convocation with the Marty the Artist family, was going to prove only half true. Kidnapped, Sally was; ransomed she was not. Death on Roe Island was the plan all along. A double revenge by the ugly green sisters: one for Sally's intrusion, one for the death of the former green right under Frank Kaiser's own dock.

Kaiser is an enigma to *sapiens* and sturgeons alike. He sells killer bait and tackle while he lecturers against the killing of undersized youngsters and oversized breeders, white or green. He sells a "how to catch 'em" book while he rails against taking more than you can eat.

Carpenter admits that Kaiser knows more about us sturgeon than anyone, including himself.

And there have been rumors that he too has the talent of conversation. None of my clan, other than our infamous brother, have ever ventured down to the San Rafael territory to find out.

Maybe Kaiser could help me and Mom. If Carpenter could get free of his unwilling anchorage, he could pontoon down through the Carquinez Straits, head northwest up across San Rafael Bay and find him. Dock A, Lochness Marina. Maybe half a day's travel, depending on the tides and the wind. Half a day back.

I shut my eyes so tight that a tear squeezed from each. I curled up and clenched my four barbels like the legs of an octopus around an abalone. I blew air backwards through my nostrils (it hurt, don't try it) to cut out the smell sense—I couldn't have smelled a live ghost shrimp if it was perched on my snout. I prayed to *Somesturgeon,* and I recited six stanzas of Hiawatha chanting "Mische Nahma, Mische Nahma" with reverent emphasis, and I thought KAISER, KAISER, KAISER, KAISER so hard that I blacked out.

When I came to, it was still daytime—how many hours had passed I couldn't tell. The green guards were still there, eating grass shrimps. One shark remained, sucking the brains out of the distended head of a king salmon. Maybe it was noon, maybe supper time. No food was offered me. I listened for the sound of beers opening. It was dead quiet on the surface. Had Carpenter gotten my thought and freed his craft of the anchor chain, escaping toward Fraser's headquarters? Or had he simply, and finally, run out of brew?

I had dreams worse than the night back on Steamboat Slough when Carpenter had left me alone. That nightmare of a whale-inhaling sized giant squid was replaced by kaleidoscopic visions of Gloria Green planting barb-less, rusty, metal fishhooks into my mom's soft under-belly. She'd poke one in and wiggle it, back and forth, then thrust it deeper, all the way to the shank. Then grab another from a basket held by the bitch sister, and start the torture anew. Blood oozed from fifty cavities, clouding the water crimson. Baby sharks were licking at the open wounds, sucking bay water made tasty with my mother's life blood, nosing the hooks in farther, or sideways, intensifying the torture.

When I woke up I was sweating. That may be hard to believe; I couldn't believe it myself. And I was crying. My fins were shaking, my gizzard dry as a bone. My mother—the Sally Sturgeon, the noblest fish of the ancients, the one loved by creatures below and above water as well, the one who had been gifted a peculiar talent through *Somesturgeon* by none other than Mische Nahma herself—was about to die.

Gloria Green returned for another visit. "How do you like your quarters here, my dear?"

she gurgled. "Sleeping well, are we? It's nearly low tide, nearly time for the festivities. Won't your mom be surprised when she sees you. Wonder which of you should be forced from the water first? I'll ask my sister. Hey, hey, hey; water to land, water to air, what a fitting end for a white," she cackled as she left.

Only hours left. I thought of my nieces and nephews, and Delores and Dirk, and Arlene and Aretha. Of all the little Es that I was hoping to name. Of garlic sautéed crawdad tails prepared by Marty the Artist at splendid Fourth of July picnics, little Winslow floating about Steamboat Slough on his Styrofoam kick board. Of how much I loved my mom.

"Don't know him by name, but I sure as shit saw him that day," said Frank Kaiser to Carpenter. "Kicked the crap out of an old green who'd lived here for years. Old green apparently said something derogatory about the kid's mom, and the kid went right after him. Wasn't really a fair fight, the age difference and all. Lots of sturgeon around here were upset about it. I try and stay out of the piscine squabbles. Got enough trouble selling invisible ghost shrimps on a hook; some of my customers are real doubters."

"Seen the kid lately?" asked Carpenter, adding, "His name is Arlie; he's the first born son of Sally Sturgeon."

"Sally's kid? You got to be kidding! I thought Sally's clan was a gentle lot. Arlie is a product of Sally?"

"Speculation is he's a product on the sperm side of a descendent of old Bentley, the sturge who the island in Miner Slough is created on top of."

"Heard the story. Some guy tried to get me to sell copies of it a few years back. Lived up on the Sacramento someplace. No matter. How can I help you, Mr. Carpenter?"

"If we can find Arlie, I figure we can take him back up to Roe Island and have him bust up the gang of greens holding Sally and her daughter, Miss B, hostage," Carpenter explained.

"From the sight of his fight here, I'd say you're right on that count," said Kaiser. "And I know right where he is, though I don't know how to get him to go with you. They say you talk to sturgeon. That right, Carpenter?"

"Maybe I can, maybe I can't. I've spent considerable time with Sally, got to know her ways. I hear the same about you. That you got the gift too."

"Some say that. Don't like to talk about it much. People look at you funny when they hear you can converse with a sturgeon."

"Know the feeling," said Carpenter, nodding his head and smiling. "How about it. Can you get Arlie to go with me?"

"If it will save Sally, I'll do it. But let's keep this between me and you, OK? Arlie and me'll meet you at the end of the pier in ten minutes. Grab a couple gallons of those olives on your way; they may come in handy."

"I also need a new anchor," said Carpenter.

"Take as many as you want. There's a pile of them on the dock by the fuel pumps. And Carpenter, I get a real thirst-on when I'm boating the bay. Get plenty of beer."

"Know the feeling," said Carpenter.

The guards had taken me outside the rusted hulk of a jail and swum me toward shore. We laid there for an hour. I was surrounded by a dozen greens, the sharks apparently having been sent away on another task. I wasn't blindfolded—what would be the point?—and I wasn't offered a final cigarette or cigar. Sturgeon are quiet fond of cigars, but our lack of teeth make the traditional biting-off of the tip nearly impossible.

Then she appeared. Or rather, suddenly I could sense her familiar smell. "Mom?"

"B?" she responded.

Another school of greens brought her beside me and quickly herded us to even shallower water. We were no more than five feet from the edge of land and air. And death.

"What are you doing here, B?"

"It's a long story Mom. Are you OK?"

"I'm fine sweetheart."

"Mom," I whispered, "Carpenter came with me and I think he has gone to get help. Remember that guy Kaiser, the *sapien* king of the sturgeon?"

"The one who helped Carpenter's weird friend Alex save all the Delta sturgeon from destruction?"

"That's the guy. I told Carpenter to go get him."

"Sweetheart, you can't tell Carpenter anything. You can't talk to *sapiens,* dearest."

"Mom, you won't believe it, but I'm special like you. Different though. I discovered that I can <u>think</u> to *sapiens,* at least to Carpenter."

"Well, we are quite a family, aren't we?"

"But it's all going to be wasted unless Carpenter and Kaiser and. . ."

"And who, B?"

"And. . . maybe. . . Arlie show up to save us."

"My little boy Arlie? You think. . . you think he'll come help?"

"I hope so Mom. Even with his troubles, I'm sure he loves you very much. You are the most special sturgeon in all the waters of the earth, you know. You are the only Sally Sturgeon."

With that, we were pulled apart and she was pushed the final few feet toward the Roe Island shore. She spun around, chastising the school of greens with "I will fin to shore on my own, thank you," and turned to do so, with the dignity that you would expect, head held high.

As I cried a final "I love you Mom," there was a huge commotion behind me. Greens were scattering everywhere. Even my six guards abandoned their post. I nudged my way backwards, spun tail to head, and finned toward the ruckus in deeper water. I saw the bottom of Carpenter's pontoon boat, heard his voice and that of another. And, though it had been so long, oh so long, I immediately recognized the scent of my older brother. The greens seemed in full retreat.

I started to rise to the surface to see Carpenter, but back-to-back pops of beer cans told me he and a companion were OK. No need to embarrass Carpenter with fish talk in front of a *sapien* friend. The trusty Yamaha gave a roar and they were off, heading in the direction of San Rafael. It was suddenly very quiet. I sank to the bottom, still trembling with fear, the horror of the past days heavy upon me.

Something nudged me from behind. I leapt from the silt and raced off like *Somesturgeon* the ancient. Something piscine was chasing me, yelling words I ignored. It was nearly upon me, so I finned ever harder and I tailed ever stronger, chanting a Mische Nahma mantra, driven by the thought of yet another green nightmare.

From behind I finally heard it say: "Hey, slow down, it's only me." It was Arlie. I stopped and he pulled along side so I could see him.

"You scared me! I thought you were a green. Are they still around?"

"Dozens of them, and are they ever pissed," said Arlie. "We fooled them for a few minutes. Carpenter spun the pontoon boat in circles full throttle, bouncing six anchors off the bottom. Luckily, one anchor ripped open the belly of a green. That distracted the sharks; they went to work immediately— with them, instinct is everything. And Kaiser heaved those special green olives—the ones from Corning that he uses to bait up the invisible ghost shrimps rigs—into the water by the hundreds. That distracted the greens. And I swam back and forth through them all so fast that they must have thought every white in the Delta had come to the rescue."

"I just heard Carpenter's pontoon boat leave. He can't help us anymore."

"I know. We've got to get out of here right now, and fast. Follow me and don't look back."

"But what about Mom?" I asked.

"I don't know where she is, sis," Arlie replied.

"But maybe she's stuck on the shore—half in and half out."

"She's on her own. Let's go sis."

"But she might be drowning in air on the land."

"Smell that?" he replied. "Here come the greens. We gotta go."

We've lived under Kaiser's dock since the escape. I miss Steamboat Slough and my sisters and nieces and nephews, but it's not so bad here. I've got Arlie.

The scuttlebutt from our white friends in the bay is that a troop of greens is still up near Roe Island, lurking in ambush, waiting for one of us to make a move back up The River. We haven't tried.

There's been no word from Carpenter. He hasn't visited, and if he has inquired about us to the *sapien* in the bait shop above, we've never heard. The *sapien* here in San Rafael doesn't come down to talk with Arlie and me. Not even on Sundays, like Carpenter used to do with our mom. Maybe this *sapien* is more afraid than Carpenter of the land-locked padded cell that Mom once told me about.

There's been no word of her. No one has seen her since the kidnapping. If she's dead, probably no one would want to tell us. Maybe she's dead.

If only Carpenter and Fraser and Arlie had arrived to Roe Island sooner. Like I said, the men in Mom's life have been nothing but trouble. Nothing but trouble.

FORREST'S BIRTHDAY

A friend's child is named Forrest, appropriate to the geography where the friend conceived him—the Sierra Nevada foothills, Nevada City. Another's is River, for equally valid reasons, though less by an act of love as for the love of the act of conceiving.

River is today six. A party took place beginning at noon, the participants dispensed promptly at three. An unpopped balloon became untied and rose to the interface of mammal and fish, where it is now floating in small, irregular circles, held against the current by the swirl of a back-eddy.

River is cranky, restless, hyped from oily smelt and crawdad snacks. River has a tangled cache of birthday-past now tucked safely in a depression in the silt behind the sunken cottonwood that washed down on last spring's flood to where they live: east bank, above Bright Bend, opposite Ski Beach. One youngster gifted a blue heron egg, unhatched. Uncle proudly gave a still-shiny, silver Broken-Back Rebel lure, which he caught trolling on too weak a line the year of River's hatch; saved until this coming-out, six floods later. River's sister shared a collection of clam shells, arranged in descending size so as to fit into them-selves, a puzzle box: open the clam, find a clam; open the next, find another; the azure pebble surprise coming after twelve repeats.

Catfish neighbors had come by. Pile worm gifts. Nice enough. Properly shared—*watch your manners, River*—with his party friends, devoured before the candles were lit and blown.

An anadromous steelhead trout, one of the first of the winter-run, had pulled in to rest nearby. River said: "hello." Trout finned over, joining the ghost shrimp lunch out of polite-ness, unaccustomed to the texture or the taste of the translucent crustacea. No present to give, advice instead: don't wander downstream below the Delta. Men swilling beer on boats with depth-finders and fish-indicators and hundred pound-test lines multihooked, armed with gaffs and inescapable nylon nets, will slaughter you there. Stay here, River; go up, River, should you need to breed or explore or vacation. A valuable present indeed, to be saved not behind the sunken cottonwood, but in River's mind. Perhaps—in a hundred generations—in his 240 chromosomes.

A *sapien* who lived upriver—and brooked (at least, so it was said) none of his neighbor's sturgeon slaughter habits—had also drifted by. He was known to River's aunt Sally, the one from Steamboat Slough an hour downstream. The man anchored above the festivities on a platform of plywood held afloat by two aluminum pontoons, drifting into the spot motor-off, courteous. River had enjoyed his boat before, nudging and mouthing the dangling electronic sensors often, fooling the sapien as to the parameters of speed and depth. The man always laughed when River played this trick. River liked his good humor, and so he welcomed him to the birthday party. The man told River of Forrest, birthdaying likewise today, but up past the Feather River, up further than the Yuba, up finally into the brook called Deer Creek which boiled and cascaded and riffled shallow near Forrest's home.

But now—the trout tourist and the neighboring catfish and the visiting pontooned man gone—River had become cranky. His mother cleaned up the party debris and put him down to nap.

The man napped too, back at his dock, between River and Forrest. He dreamed that the two met. It was a future dream, both boys old. Himself, the mothers, the aunt all dead. That the two met one day where the Yuba meets the Feather, where the sturgeon could breed in a redd of clear water around boulders and gravel, in the soft shadows of trees grown tall, uncut.

THE PONTOON'S STORY

"OH how many timEs were you sEEn
amOng the waVeS of the gReat swOLLen oCean,
looming like a mOUntaiN,
d e f e A t i n g and overwHelmiNg them,
and wiTh your bLAck and bRistLy baCk
             furrOwing the sea wateRs,
and with sTAtely and g r A v E bearing!"

Leonardo da Vinci, *Codex Atlanticus*, folio 265.

) was beat up. Especially my bottom. My outboard friend was pooped. Particularly her second cylinder. I figured we both deserved a good rest. That last adventure with Sally and Carpenter was a killer.

Carpenter apparently agreed, for he'd left the two of us on top of The River, down the bank from his and Janie's house which sits on the inside of the Garden Highway levee; the Yamaha 30-horse bolted to me, me roped to the dock, all three of us left to rise and fall with the foot-high wakes of passing multi-cabin, double-diesel cruisers late of, or going to, the Delta; left to roll on the ripples of low slung ski boats cleanly carving the early morning flat and calm; left to nap through the wakeless vibration of aluminum skiffs trolling against the current, trailing lures and flashers aimed at salmon and stripers.

At first I was glad. The past year had seen a lot of nautical miles pass under my twin hulls. Heck, I'd been back and forth to Sally Sturgeon's place—at Steamboat Slough, downriver from here—a half dozen times. I'd been part way up the Feather River—though abandoned when she got too shallow, as you may have heard—on that crazy multiplication expedition that Sally convinced Carpenter and me to participate in so she could get laid in a clear water tributary amongst though not by another sturgeon specie. It caused a great hullaballo amongst The River's inhabitants, but Carpenter, my owner, was nonplussed, as usual.

And then there was that trip down below the Delta—the Roe Island fiasco. Hell, me and the Yamaha had to race all the way to San Rafael and back twice, in that battle with the evil green sturgeon. Over and back, over and back. Do you know how far that is? No wonder my bottom still itches: all that dang San Francisco Bay salt water chaffing by at fifteen knots, hour after hour.

But after three weeks of floating at home, I was bored. Moss and scum were taking up residence on my aluminum pontoon bottoms, and the top of the prop of the Yamaha had collected a half-inch of silt plus a family of clams. One of the two ropes holding me in place had come loose and the past weekend had been a nightmare: my right side banged Mr. Dock's left from dawn till dusk from what must have been a thousand ski boats racing by. I felt bad for Mr. Dock, but all I could do was wait for Carpenter's return.

By the fourth week, I still hadn't seen hide nor hair of him. Not like him to stay away. Used to be he'd come down and sit on me nearly every day, sipping beers and fussing with all the altimeter, compass, and fish finder-type gadgets he'd installed on, in and under me. Used to fuss and sip for hours on end. But now he'd disappeared. Just like his friend Sally.

I mentioned my inanimate compatriots, the motor and the dock. I've always gotten along pretty well with the neighborhood animates too, *Homo sapiens* and *Acipenser transmontanus* alike. I liked Carpenter (he's the *sapien*) soon as he bought me; he's always treated me pretty good (though not so good just right now). And as to Sally (she's the *transmontanous*); well, who <u>wouldn't</u> like the most famous sturgeon in The River? (I know, I know—the green sturgeon, the *A. medirostris*, and especially their bitch-queen Gloria, Gloria Green, that's who.) Sally Sturgeon: grand-daughter of old Ossian, the famous teller of fish tails. Great grand-daughter of older-still Winslow, so old that he actually witnessed the arrival of catfish to The River. Aquaintance of Alex, Carpenter's crazy friend who saved the sturgeon from extinction at the hands (and poles, rods, reels, lines, lures, nets, gaffs, and hooks) of *sapien* fishermen by concocting the invisible ghost shrimps bait trick. That Sally Sturgeon is something. What an honor to have known her.

I was going nuts. Night after night of moon-shines waxing and waning on The River's back; the tide ebbing and rising, ebbing and rising. (Yes, I can feel it up here in The River; surprised?). Day after day of bobbing up and down; barnacles and algae and scum and silt collecting on me like a Dutra family barge. Week after week of fading and warping and peeling in the mid-summer scorcher Central Valley heat.

I was bored stiff as the steel girders on the new Southport Bridge. Finally I screamed "Where the hell *is* everybody anyway?" as loud as I could. My words bounced between the levee banks until they fell onto The River and were swept downstream, clinging to the backs of wavelettes and backeddies, riding their way seaward. And no others came back.

Next morning, when the crest of the sun snuck over the lip of the levee, I saw that a third of the local inanimates had disappeared. No, someone hadn't stolen the Yamaha off my stern. It was the dock. There wasn't plank nor nail of him in sight. Huh? Someone had stole my dock pal right from under my prow. Oh, boy; Carpenter's gonna be pissed, I thought. Late night dock-thieves, that's all we need.

Sun full-up, I looked around. I was down at Bryte Bend across the levee from Broderick. I felt kinda stupid: dock-stealers, indeed.

Having been down this water before, I knew the Virgin Sturgeon floating bar and grill was soon to arrive. And that the fleet of paddlewheeler tourist boats (whose paddlewheels turn only from the headway produced by a pair of many-horse outboard motors secreted astern) moored at the docks of Old Sacramento weren't far downstream.

Guess the second of the two ropes gave up, I said to the Yamaha. She didn't say anything back, but I was sure she was pleased to be out in the current where the deposit of silt would gradually wash from her prop.

Old Sacramento disappeared from my bow (we were drifting backwards just then, though we'd been going frontwards and sideways too, lacking any *sapien* guidance). It was a pleas-ant morning, a gentle Delta breeze in the air. After the extended sabbatical at Carpenter's place, it was nice to gander at the marinas and other *sapien* structures clinging to and piled upon the levees as they floated past. Nice too to see my animate friends—the cottonwoods and willows—waving from the same banks as they passed me. I wished I could wake back.

Morning passed into afternoon and Miller Park passed us. Then the Sacramento Yacht Club (I heard they don't let the likes of me moor at the place), Sherwood Harbor, DaRosa Marina, Loris Bros. Marina, Four Seasons Marina, Light 29 Marina, Bud's Bait & Tackle, Freeport Marina & Bait Shop, Cliff's Marina. Near dusk and nearly to Courtland, a Sheriff Patrol boat came by. Seeing me captain and crew-less, the water-borne deputies towed me to the west bank. They figured me for a nocturnal navigation accident waiting to happen; and they were right, for I had no way to turn on the night lights, that being a *sapien* task. Given that collision is a two-party affair, I cooperated fully.

It was a pretty decent spot. I was roped to an old piling, and the piling was in an eddy, and that kept me from bumping and scraping the rocked bank during the night. Didn't need no dang rocking and banging just now; no thank you.

Night passed into morning and a small tug (like pile-driver John Lucas of Clarksberg uses to tow around his pile-driving barge) pulled aside. Some *sapiens* hopped aboard me and switched the rope from the piling to their craft. Great! I thought; Carpenter must've finally come home, found his dock pontoon boat-less, and sent these guys to the rescue. Ooh-whee! It will be a nice tow back upstream. Home sweet home! I can see him now, standing on the dock, beer in hand; concerned, caring, anxious to hop on my back, curious as to the health of his nautical gadgets, eager for the Yamaha's putt-putt and purr, ready to gently reunite me and Mr. Dock with some brand new, store-bought, shiny yellow nylon ropes, yack-yack-yacking plans for another great River adventure. Ooh whee, I can just see him now.

Yikes! It was suddenly dark. A tarpulin. They'd tossed a dang tarpulin over my rails, and now we were moving. And I could tell from the flow of The River on my aluminum pontoon bottom that we weren't going upstream. Down instead. Dang it, what's up? Couple hours later we stopped and I got the oddest sensation. Very aerial. A sense of aboveness. It's hard to describe: I hadn't been out since I was fabricated, and that had been nearly twenty years prior.

I was up in the air, no doubt about it. Dang it. Swinging so's I was nearly airsick. Whoa there, I'd yelled at the crane. Then I was dropped to the ground: plunk. Ground—now there's a *really* wierd feeling if you'd been waterborne for twenty years. Sure, I'd banged a few banks in my day, and I'd scraped a watery bottom my share of times (mostly on Sally Sturgeon adventures with Carpenter at the helm!). But never an up-in-the-air, thud-to-the-earth deal like this one! Dang that crane.

Then it got ugly.

I'd be exaggerating if I said it was painful. After all, I'm only inanimaticity: mostly aluminum, a little dead wood, few hunks of brass and steel, a tad plastic.

But it wasn't pleasant.

How would you feel . . . how would you explain . . . no, how would you *describe*. . . being disassembled? Huh?

[The following is excerpted from a notebook found in a trash barrel on the public beach at Tahoe City, summer of 1995. The notebook apparently belonged to a University student majoring in Historical Hydrocartography.]

In searching for the *true headwater* of The River on this last road trip, a number of true facts were collected well. Facts about Goose Lake, the two forks of the Pit River, the streams of Mt. Eddy, the bubbling spring in the city park of the City of Mt. Shasta. Others were collected in contradiction, like facts about Shasta Dam. Take the volume of the dam. One handout from the Information Desk of the Visitor's Center at Shasta Dam listed earth and concrete at 2,160,000 and 6,270,000 cubic yards, respectively. Another: 11,975,000 tons of aggregate and 6,757,500 barrels of cement. I don't doubt that these volumes and masses of inorganic substances once tallied correctly into the one heck of a big hunk of dam at Shasta. But by the time I got there, it had gotten smaller. I have proof, having hauled home about twenty pounds of it: four concrete cylinders—each about a foot long, four inches in diameter—cored out of the dam in the course of a routine inspection of its integrity, and placed in a wooden bin in the parking lot near the Visitor's Center with a sign that read *Shasta Dam Concrete Core Samples—Take One*, which I did, for my six year old friend and neighbor Matthew, for a future school show-and-tell project (how many kids do you know who have a verified, authentic chunk of Shasta Dam?), plus three more to spare. The sample bin was nearly empty when I pulled my mementos in September. That was after the height of the tourist season, so who knows how many *tons* of little five pound cores were taken home to grandchildren, elementary school teachers or barkeeps that summer? Worst still, a display at the Visitor's Center showed James Cone and Dave Pryor—the first two humans (with government approval) to rappel down the face of the dam—examining a pock-mark on said face caused by the dislodgment of a considerable chunk of dam later located (in pieces) in the river below and estimated to be between 3800 and 7350 pounds. But I don't wish to quibble about a few pounds here and there. Like you would see if you went there, it's one big fat mother of a dam.

I asked Bill Mauck, the guy behind the Information Desk, to help me with some facts presented on the Daily Information Board. The fact that the Daily Information Board was dated the day prior was troublesome, but I figured that one day couldn't matter much to a 4,552,000 acre-foot reservoir. (An acre-foot is enough water to cover an acre of land one foot deep; if you ever try to do this, please remember that you have to cover the acre *really fast* or some of the feet of water will soak into the acre and mess up the measurement.) In addition to yesterday's facts (the date, temperature, water depth at the dam, outlet flow, &c.), the Daily Information Board noted certain important historical minimums and maximums, like the distance of the lake surface from "the crest." The record low was on 14 September 1977: 230.32 feet below "the crest." Depending where you look it up, "the crest" is 1077.5 feet or 1065.0 feet or 1037.0 feet above the Pacific Ocean. It's also above the Sacramento River, which rages from an intentional hole in the bottom of the dam into the canyon 500 more or less feet below. The record high was on 25 May 1982 at 0.06 inches below the crest.

"Bill, what does this mean here, *the crest*?" I asked, pointing to the board.

"That's the top of the dam," said Bill.

"The top of the spill gates?"

"No, the top of the dam."

"Which top of the dam? The top of the actual structure?"

"No, the top of the roadway on top of the dam."

"Has water ever gone on top of the top of the roadway on top of the dam?"

"No, of course not. That would not be safe. We always keep the water safely below the top."

"Bill, you're telling me that this one fact here (I'm pointing to it) on your Daily Information Board dated yesterday is correct and that the water once reached six *hundredths* of an inch from the very, very tippy-top of the dam? Isn't that cutting it a little close?"

"Well within our safety margin, sir. Can I help the next person?"

Shasta Dam was built somewhere between the late 30's and the afternoon of 17 June 1950, when a "ceremonial spill" (over the spillway, not the roadbed) was performed for an assemblage of assorted dignitaries. A piece of propaganda titled *The Central Valley Project*, written by the Workers of the Writer's Program of the Work Project Administration and published midway through the dam's construction by the California State Department of Education in 1942, notes that the first concrete was poured on 8 July 1940. At 10:02 a.m. Most of the rest of the book explains why this dam will be good for you. The opinions of sturgeon and salmon were not mentioned.

I was strewn about the construction yard. Some of my parts, like the plywood sheets that were once my deck, had already been dumpstered. The bulk of me—the twin aluminum pontoons—was in two places.

One pontoon was in the shade of a cottonwood tree out in the yard. It wasn't so bad there. The boat-repair *sapiens* had scrapped and polished its bottom, and it was cool in the shade, though not as cool as when it was in The River. I imagined it sitting on a set of blocks out in the full sun on an August Delta day. You wouldn't want to touch it, not after noon. "Yikes!" you'd've said.

My other one was in a shed. Had been for about a week. I don't really want to talk about what went on in there. It's over and done with now. It was like you going to the dentist for a root canal. "Ouch!" you'd've said.

My Yamaha companion was clamped to a saw horse next to the shed. The *sapiens* had drained and replenished her fluids, sharpened her propeller, replaced her three spark plugs, and polished her top so she shined brand-spanking new. They tried her out in a 55-gallon drum of water. Varroom, varroom, she went. "Ooh whee! What a good-lookin' outboard!" you'd've said.

You know all the electronical stuff Carpenter had spend all that time installing on my top? Well, guess what? All of it except the altimeter went in the trash barrel. Only the altimiter and the sturgeon listening device—the upside-down blue funnel duct-taped to the piece of garden hose that he'd lay on the water, sticking the open hose end to his ear, so's he wouldn't have to lie on his belly to converse with Sally—survived. I couldn't believe it. All them electronicals junked. "Waste of money," you'd've said.

Pretty soon I was all back together. New deck, like I'd hoped. Glossy white railings. Shiny pair of pontoons—one like before, one changed. Changed to have a fish tank inside. Fish tank with a plastic top so that a *sapien* on my new deck could see down in it, and whatever was down in it could see up at the *sapien* (or the sky, or the stars, or a passing egret; whatever).

And pretty soon I was on top of a trailer on top of a road on top of a levee, going way faster than I'd ever gone atop The River, bouncing and bumping behind a white van. On the back of the van (maybe on the sides too, I couldn't tell) was stenciled MARTY STANLEY— FINE ART—RYDE, CALIFORNIA. I recognized a couple of marinas as they zipped past. Then came a bridge, the Tower Bridge. That meant we were near Sacramento. Though land-borne and trailered, at least I was heading in the right direction. Behind a van owned by Carpenter's best pal.

I'd seen the tippy-top of the white marble spire *sapiens* call the Taylor Monument many times from The River. Carpenter's next door neighbor kids loved to go on me for trips up to it on warm summer evenings. Carpenter would tie me to a willow on the rip-rapped bank, and the kids and he would scamper up it, cross the road (South River Road, the *sapiens* call it) and try to decipher the indentations. Carpenter'd spent a whole afternoon there once, completing the transcription of the hundred-plus year old, weather-beaten, chiseled inscription. It read:

ERECTED
to the memory of
LEONIDAS TAYLOR
born in the city of
Philadelphia on the
3d. of July 1832.
He grew to manhood in the
City of St. Louis and was
killed by the explosion of the
Steamer Belle opposite this
spot on the 5th, of Feb.
1856;
His body was never found.
But distant from those who
loved him, the waters of the
Sacramento will not own
him till that day when the
sea shall give up its dead.

Carpenter and the kids had gone to the Sacramento Library after that (without me, of course) and found a news account of the tragedy. It read:

```
STEAMER EXPLODES; MANY LIVES LOST.  Sacramento, Feb. 5, 1856.
One of the worst riverboat disasters in California history occurred
today when the steamboat Belle, bound for Red Bluff, exploded
opposite the Russian Ford, 11 miles from here.  It is estimated that
as many as 30 passengers and crew members were lost in the accident.
The entire boat, with the exception of some 40 feet of the aft
portion, sank immediately.  The steamer General Reddington, on the
downward trip, reached the scene shortly after the blast and took
care of the survivors.  Capt. Charles H. Houston of the Belle is
among those known to have been killed.  Among the injured is the
well known Major John Bidwell of Chico.
```

It was fun to see the whole hunk of granite, base to tip. I was starting to enjoy the freedom of being landed. Me and the trailer and the van stayed on the gravel edge of the water side of the levee road while Marty the Artist and his darling wife Sherry, their son Winslow packed on her back, crawled down the bank to The River. Marty the Artist had grabbed Carpenter's famous sturgeon-listening device from one of my shiny-new, verathaned plywood deck boxes, and he'd propped Winslow with it on a boulder at The River's edge. Winslow was alternately yelling at The River and then listening to it by holding the hose end of the listening contraption to his ear.

Sherry came back up, opened the sliding side door (I could hear it) and slid back down the bank again, cradling a watermelon. Must be a snack for little Winslow, I yelled to the Yamaha outboard motor bolted to my stern. As usual, the Yamaha didn't reply. Probably occupied with the new scenery—the Taylor spire, the walnut fields, the distant Sutter Buttes—like I was.

A loud "kerplop" turned my attention back to the assemblage on the bank. Sherry had heaved her melon into The River. I remembered hearing Carpenter retelling the watermelon story that Sally's great grandpa Ossian, the famous teller of fish tails, had told her, and she, in turn, had told him. Carpenter him. About a trainload of watermelons that had derailed into The River. About how watermelons were the sturgeon's favorite fruit.

A loud "Sally!!" got my attention again. "Sally, Sally." It was Winslow, yelling across the water. And there she was, just downstream: head out of the water, gray diamond-shaped scutes gleaming in the sunlight, parcels of The River dripping from her dangling barbels, her proboscis smiling toothless. Holy Carp! I'd figured her for a goner after the fight with the greens down at Roe Island. Oh buoy! Wait till Carpenter hears about this! If we can ever find him.

Sally finned over to the bank and treaded against the current, a rod's length away from Winslow. He'd picked up a few words of sturgeonese from Carpenter over the years, and you could see that he and Sally were trying to communicate. Of course I couldn't hear her words, but occasionally her tail wagged sideways, or her head bobbed up and down, in cross-specie gestures anyone could see were nos and yesses. While Winslow yelled his few simple sturgeon verbs and nouns toward her, Marty the Artist pointed and waved upriver. Transmissions completed, Sally sank from sight and the *sapien* threesome scampered back up the bank and into the van. We were off down the road heading north alongside The River in no time at all.

Just past the big I-5 bridge and across from the infamous Alamar Marina (I'd parked there many a time while Carpenter and his pals chugged afternoon bottles of Coors—boy, were *those* rides home ever something!) was the weeded and brushy outline of the former ramp of the now abandoned, pre-I5, Elkhorn Ferry. I was soon bumping down it, Yamaha-end first.

When my pontoons touched that water, well . . . well, I thought I'd died and joined Poseidon's paradise—that wonderful, aqueous kingdom-come.   When I'd slid all the way in and felt that coolness; when my bottom became immersed in the caressing gentleness of The River's soothing, watery arms; when I was rocked back and forth by the current; well, well . . . there's just no *sapien* words to describe it.

And when Marty the Artist fired up the Yamaha and the *varoom, varooom, varo o o o m s* rattled my aluminum frame, it felt like old Neptune himself was giving me a backrub.

But the best of it all was just after Marty propped open the clear plastic top of the new tank built into my left pontoon. Sally finned alongside and, with a triple wag of her tail, hopped into me.

"Hi old friend," she said.

"Its good to have you back Sally Sturgeon," I said. "Are you cumfy in there?"

"It's not too bad. Little crowded, but I don't think the trip will be too long."

"What trip?" I asked.

"No one told you? We're going to Lake Shasta. Driving right around that dam damn, since I can't swim up, over or through it."

"I understand the dam part, but why Lake Shasta?"

"So I can swim up the Upper Sacramento to the big spring in the City Park of Mt. Shasta City. The big spring that the Mt. Shasta City Chamber of Commerce claims as the headwaters of The River. The headwater claim is nothing but bait for source-of-The River-challenged tourists. But it's a *known* fact amongst fishes and waters alike that the mouth of that spring connects directly to Pyramid Lake over in Nevada through a tunnel right under the Sierra mountains. It's a water tunnel that lets the moving waters who drop from the clouds onto the *east* side of the Sierra get back, sooner or later, to the Pacific Ocean. Didn't you ever hear Carpenter talk about it? It's one of his favorite hydrocartographic stories."

"I don't know," I said. "He talks about a lot of silly stuff. Maybe I lost some memory when Marty the Artist had me refabricated."

"Thanks to my best of all daughters, Miss B," said Sally.

"Miss B? What's she got to do with this?"

"Dearest Pontoon. She's the one who undid you from the dock. And she's the one who asked Winslow Stanley to convince his dad to come rescue you and get you all fixed up for this adventure. I must say that you do look quite handsome with that new deck and all."

"Oh, thanks. Wish we knew where Carpenter was so he could see me."

"I'll be seeing him soon enough. That's the whole point to this trip. According to Marty the Artist, he's in seclusion at his cabin above Truckee. Won't come home to The River. Thinks I died at Roe Island, died at the fins of the evil green sturgeon. He's been in mourning for two months. Won't talk to anyone, not even Marty the Artist or Janie. They say it's so bad that he's even stopped writing those absolutely true historical pieces about The River and the fantasies of its inhabitants."

"Geeze, that's awful," I said.

"So I'm going to go through the tunnel from the Shasta spring over to Pyramid Lake, swim up the Truckee River to the confluence of Trout Creek—which isn't a creek, it's a brook, but no matter—and further up Trout Whatever to his cabin to see him. Prove to him I'm still alive. Talk him into coming back home. Marty the Artist and Janie think I'm the only one he'll listen to."

"Do I get to come along?" I asked.

"You're too big, Mr. Pontoon. I heard that Marty the Artist is going to haul you over to Lake Tahoe after you drop me off at Lake Shasta. I think he's donated you to some foundation run by that limnology guy from the big school at Davis. Charley Silverstein. No, that's not right. Arlie Goldfarb. No, Arlie's my son's first name. Maybe it's Farley . . ."

"Arlie, Charley, Farley, barnacaley, who cares," I interrupted. "I've heard it's cold at Lake Tahoe."

"Talk to Marty the Artist about it, there's nothing I can do."

"You know those *sapiens* won't listen to me. Even my Yamaha ignores me. You're the only one who talks to me."

"I'm sorry Pontoon, I really am. We've all got our troubles. Look, we're about to leave so you need to hush up. I hear it's real flat and boring from here to Redding, so I'm planning on a nice long nap. And Pontoon: please stay on the trailer, will you?"

Flat and boring was right. And hot. Though I don't mind hot. It's always hot in the Sacramento Valley, even on The River. I like hot. Not like that Tahoe place. Dang it, I'll get buried in snow and won't be able to see a thing. My aluminum welds are gonna crack and I'll sink. Snap, crackle, pop; bubble, bubble, bubble. I'll probably get crushed by an iceberg. Ooh-whee: icebergs. I just know that lake is full'a humongous icebergs. What a way to go. O o h w h e e .

The fish jumped several times and the third time it came up, it danced on its tail across the water like a marlin. —Joey Pallotta, describing the catch of his record (468 pound, 9'6") white sturgeon in the lower Sacramento River near Carquinez Straits, 7 June 1983.

Turns out these Lake Tahoe folks are a pretty nice bunch. They rented me an inside berth at the marina in front of Jake's Restaurant On The Lake at Tahoe City. They already own two other boats; one's a hefty commercial trawler-type boat with a pair of grunting diesel inboard engines and a covered place for the driver, complete with a steering wheel. What'll these *sapiens* think of next!

Turns out there aren't any icebergs. Not even in winter, one of the other boats told me.

Marty the Artist towed me Sally-less up here right after our mission at Lake Shasta. You should see the trees. Ooh-wee. They are way prettier than my willow and cottonwood friends down on The River—but please, don't tell them I said so.

Marty the Artist turned me over to the limnologist guy and his team of aqueous scientists. He knows Carpenter from some school down in the valley where The River flows. The students call him The Professor; the rest of the *sapiens* call him Doc.

The *sapiens* in general have called Lake Tahoe a bunch of names, according to one of the students here. On Valentine's Day in 1844, explorer John Charles Fremont and map-maker Georg Carl Ludwick (Charles) Preuss took a lunch break at the top of a peak near here and became the first whites (white *sapiens,* not white sturgeon) to see The Lake. Fremont originally named it Mountain Lake, but then switched it to Lake Bonpland—in honor of some frog botanist with the same last name, but first-named Amié, not Lake —which is how it is labelled on his pal Preuss' 1848 map. In 1854, some friends of then California Governor John Bigler passed a law naming it Lake Bigler. Some non-friends unsympathetic to Bigler's support of the Confederacy switched it to Lake Tahoe in 1862, but the Democratic legislature of 1870 re-declared it Lake Bigler, which is how it stood on the official records—though nobody paid any attention and called it Tahoe anyway—until 1945. *Tah-oo* is an approximate phonetic translation of the local Washo Indian word for "lake water."

I'm not sure what the translation of *limnology* is, but the professor who purports to practice it seems like a nice old coot. He got me four brand new yellow plastic bumpers right off, so I wouldn't bash the dock. Carpenter never bought me much of anything nautical, other than all the electronical stuff that so fascinated him. All that stuff got tossed when I was rebuilt except the altimeter; this morning it read 6228 feet, two feet below the top of the six foot dam built at the Truckee River outlet by Colonel Von Schmidt in 1870. Who'd ever have thought it: me—a river, delta and bay kinda guy—being waterborne a mile high!

While I was being towed up and over the mountains, Sally should've been finning and tailing the secret tubular shortcut down and under. Don't know if she made it through to Pyramid Lake. Don't know if she made it up the Truckee River to the turnoff at Trout Creek. Hard to get any sturgeon news here at The Lake.

The final stage of her plan was to splash up Trout Creek and hail Carpenter at his cabin on the hill above Truckee town. I'm pretty sure that part would have worked. I'm pretty sure that if Carpenter didn't see her, one of his neighbors would have mentioned the presence of a six foot six, hundred ten pound sturgeon shoving its way up little Trout Creek as it wound its way through the Tahoe-Donner meadows and across various fairways of the Tahoe Donner Championship golf course, up the hill towards Carpenter's place near the fourth hole. I'm pretty sure.

Doc and his science pals held a big meeting here last week. It was called "The Tahoe Symposium on USOs." I don't know why they called it that. But I do know a USOs is. The scientists have had me out on a dozen USO surveillance missions since I got here. They mounted me with a really expensive sonar gizzmo to help with the task. It's way fancier than anything electronical that Carpenter ever stuck on me.

Somebody gave Doc a flag. It now flies from the old piece of aluminum pipe that serves as my mast. The flag has a drawing of a monster fish on it with the word "TESSIE" printed toward the bottom. Tessie, like a Tahoe Nessie. Like the mythical monster of Loch Ness. You've heard of it?

Well, some *sapiens* up here think they've got one too. *Sapiens* must think that all big lakes need monster fishes. Big, mine is. She's about twenty one miles long and thirteen wide (depends where you start and finish). She's 1647 feet deep (when her top matches that of Von Schmidt's dam). And she holds enough liquid to flood all of California more than a foot deep (though most of it would settle in the low parts, like the middle of the Sacramento Valley, like over the top of Carpenter's house). But monstered she isn't, or so I thought before the scientists took me out on my first USO cruise.

Most of the public USO sightings are phony. *Sapiens* from all around The Lake phone Doc to tell of the things they've seen, fax him those they've thought they've seen, mail him those they've dreamed they've seen, and buy another round for those they've blind-drunk sure as shit seen. Some of these people have brought Doc actual photographs and video clips. "Verified sightings," they're called.

Most of the sightings are explainable by normal science. I listened to Doc give a USO lecture to a group on my back just last week. Floating sticks and limbs, he explained. Old yellowed plastic and styrafoam, he told them. Sunset and sunrise light reflecting off waves. Mirages caused by fog rising from the surface.

Doc's favorite is the undulating wave. It's created from the freak collision of boat wakes reflected off the shores. These boat wakes, by themselves, are so gentle that you can't hardly see 'em. But when they are lined up just right and happen to meet out in the middle of

The Lake, they combine and amplify and propagage into an undulating wave that looks like a giant snake slithering vertical across the water. Science can explain *everything,* Doc is fond of saying.

Last week, a crew of student scientists climbed aboard and took me over to Emerald Bay. It's a beautiful spot, enjoyed by tourists and locals alike. The locals are both native and immigrant, but do not include any *sapiens,* for the land and water are now a California State Park. There's a little island in the middle of the bay—it's the only true island in all of Lake Tahoe—which has been called variously Cocqette, Fannette, Dead Man's, Hermit's and Emerald Isle. Two of the names came from Captain Richard Barter, the "Hermit of Emerald Bay," who lived there until his death by drowning in 1873. There's a stone "tea house" on it now, built by Mrs. Knight, the eccentric Scandinavian who had the famous *Vikingsholm* castle constructed on the mainland aside the bay in 1929.

The local natives are few: silver trout, Tahoe cutthroat, white fish. The local immigrants include landlocked salmon (Kokanee), Royal silver trout, German browns, and the dreaded Mackinaw. The Macs get a bad rep from the *sapiens* who monitor and manipulate the variety and number of fishes of The Lake. They call the Macs "cannibals" for their predilection to reduce the number of smaller, native fishes via consumption. Truth be told, most critters in The Lake eat one another.

Take sturgeon for example. There's a critter I know a lot about. Now sturgeon never ever eat *each other*—Sally swears it—but they are most certainly not vegetarians. Clams and shrimps (ghost shrimps, mud shrimps, grass shrimps) are their daily diet in The River. And when the herring spawn in San Francisco Bay, sturgies from clear up in The Delta swim over to participate. But the real mainstay of sturgeon metabolic activity is crawdads. California crayfish, some of you may call 'em. *Pacifastacus linisculus,* guys like Doc call them.

Turns out that there are crawdads aplenty in The Lake. Doc says sixty five million and rising. Adults, he adds. Sixty five thousand thousands of the pink and red crustacea, half (I assume) ready to reproduce, the other half willing to help out at a moment's notice. One hundred thirty million pinchers. Probably a billion little legs. A billion. Maybe more, counting the youngsters. If word of this ever got back to The River, sturgeon tourists would flock here in droves. If Sally had ever known of this lake-o-plenty, she'd have opened a chain of bottom-and-breakfast inns in the wiggle of a barbel.

If Sally's grand-daddy Ossian had known, he'd have concocted a *different* version of the tail of the ghost shrimps-gorging sturgeon named Bentley who once ate so many that he got stuck in Miner Slough in The Delta, sank, and became the foundation for an island that's there to this day. I've seen it. Old Ossian probably would have explained the creation of Emerald Isle in a similar fashion, substituting crawdads for shrimps.

But there are no sturgeon in Lake Tahoe, so all this crawdad, big sturgeon talk is pretty silly.

Last week, when the student scientists took me to Emerald Bay, it was our mission to collect various scientific data about The Lake. We took her temperature, measured her clarity, charted her isoclines, and scanned her depths with the fancy sonar device, looking for sunken ships and schools of fishes. The students got real excited at one point, jumping up and down on my plywood deck (thank goodness it's a new one) yelling "Tessie" at each other. One student detached my miniature mast with the new monster flag on the top and waved it back and forth like we were at a dang homecoming football game.

But there are no monster critters in Lake Tahoe, so all this Tessie talk is pretty silly.

I guess it came up when Doc finally noticed the fish tank built into my left pontoon. I'd been in his fleet for over a month, for Titanic sakes! Oh buoy, are these scientists ever flakey.

Doc phoned Marty the Artist to find out what the tank was for and I guess one question led to another. Someone in the Artist family finally spilled the beans. Maybe Doc threatened to tell everyone that little Winslow talked to sturgeon. Growing up is hard enough these days without a sturgeon stigma. Maybe Doc bribed Marty the Artist's wife Sherry with promises of iced shipments of crawdads for life, and she's the one who gave away Carpenter's sturgeon secrets. And his unlisted phone number at the cabin on the hill above Truckee.

I don't know exactly how it came about, but three days ago who should show up with Doc on the dock at the marina in front of Jakes On The Lake but Carpenter himself. In the flesh, though barely so. He looked awful. The last time he'd seen *me* was months back, back down on The River at his own dock. Just before he abandoned me for his monastic retreat to mourn his dead (he'd thought) best friend.

I was kinda nervous as he and Doc walked along the dock toward me. Was he going to be really pissed about all his electronical gadgets that had been discarded when I was rebuilt? What would happen if he didn't like my new plywood deck or the tint of my freshly painted railings? Did Sally complete her journey and connect with him up on Trout Creek? Did he know that Marty the Artist had donated me to the University, and taken a tax deduction to boot?

As he got closer, I saw he had a beer in his hand. That was a good sign; maybe he was still the same old Carpenter who'd once loved me on The River.

The pair reached my mooring and halted. Doc stood still, his arms crossed behind his back, glancing between Carpenter and me. Carpenter put one foot on my side and gently rocked me. He squatted down, rested his beer on my deck, and reached over to the lid of my new fish tank, opening and shutting it in silence. Standing again, Carpenter gave one of those manly nods to Doc, picked up his beer, took a long swig, and, as he leapt aboard, yelled: "He looks *terrific.*"

Whew. Doc joined us, showing off my new sonar contraption and the red monster flag with the TESSIE logo. Carpenter found his (my) (our) old altimeter and he gave it a gentle pat, like he needed the reassurance of something old to balance all the somethings new.

"So what do you have in mind, Professor?" Carpenter asked.

"Please, just call me Doc. Everyone else does," said Doc.

"Okay, Doc, you've already gotten my favorite and only boat, no thanks to my ex-pal Marty the Artist. Why should I do anything else to help you?"

"Now, now," said Doc, "no reason to be upset about the craft here. You have no idea how tough things are financially, back at the University, back down in the valley. Look, some guy I've never seen drives up here one day and offers to hand over a brand spanking-new boat. And to increase my modest fleet by fifty percent all I have to do is hand back an official University receipt for sixty grand for the guy's tax records. What'd you expect me to do, tell him to take the pontoon over to Pyramid Lake so those morons from that bush-league school in Reno could get it?"

"Sixty *thousand* dollars?" said Carpenter.

Uh oh, I thought.

"What do I care about the guy's personal needs? Guy said he was about to make a killing doing illustrations for some book, and he needed the tax writeoff."

"Sixty thousand clams for an eight by sixteen hunk of plywood and aluminum," Carpenter muttered, shaking his head.

Don't forget the Yamaha outboard and the altimeter, I thought. I was starting to take this personally.

"Look, Mr. Carpenter. You're an alum of the U. Don't you want your alma mater to succeed?

Look at all these wonderful students here," said Doc, waving at the group further down the dock. "Don't you want them to grow up educated?"

"Have them get educated back at the campus, for Pete's sake. Looks like a big fat excuse to hang around The Lake and avoid going to class, that's what this whole thing looks like to me. Big party, looks like to me."

"No, no, no. We're doing *very* important research here. My students have faithfully taken The Lake's temperature twice a day for two decades and recorded it all in indelible ink in spiral-bound journals. This is really important stuff. And now we're about to initiate the greatest research project of all: the USO project. Why I'll . . . humprh, err. . . I mean, the University, will be world famous."

"The USO project, you say. What the hell is a USO?" asked Carpenter.

"Ah ha, glad you asked! It's like UFO. Like Unidentified Flying Object, but a little different."

"The 'S' is for sinking?"

"Nope."

"Slimy?"

"Nope, try again."

"Must be stupid. Yeah, stupid like this whole conversation."

"Now, now. Calm down. You were getting close. Try one more time. Think about all this water, think about limnology. . ."

"What the hell *is* limnology, anyway?" Carpenter interrupted.

I felt better. I wasn't the only one who wondered.

"I'll explain later," said Doc. "Now, think aqueous. Think of animals in your own back yard, down in The River. Come on now, try harder."

"S as in sleeze ball, like that jerk Marty the Artist!"

"Oh boy. This is much more difficult than I would have thought. What was your field of study back at the University, Mr. Carpenter?"

"English Literature."

"Well that explains it. The word, dear alum, that begins with an 'S' in the middle of 'Unidentified' and 'Object' is . . ."

"SWIMMING!" yelled Carpenter.

"Very good," sighed The Professor.

Hearing a noise from the building, he entered. And when he shown the flashlight on the open tank, a monster rose from the surface and danced upon its tail. He fled...
—Professor Donald Crosby, recounting the one-night employment of a night watchman at the sturgeon breeding facility at U. C. Davis, circa. 1985.

Doc and Carpenter spent the rest of the afternoon sitting on my back, sipping on bottles of Sierra Nevada Pale Ale (in return for a significant donation, Doc had declared Sierra Nevada Pale Ale the "official beverage" of the University) and discussing the USO project.

As I'd suspected, Marty the Artist had divulged Carpenter's secret talent of sturgeon communication. Doc already knew so many over-achieving, three-digit IQ toting, double-PhD, child prodigy, creative geniuses from the University that he only feigned being impressed with Carpenter's unique skill. Doc was much more interested in the other half of the human-piscine duo: Sally.

"So, tell me: how exactly do you hear this *Acipenser transmontanus*?" asked Doc.

"Don't really want to talk about it," said Carpenter.

"Aw, come on. I'm a scientist. There's nothing to be ashamed of. I won't tell a sole about this."

"Not ashamed," said Carpenter. "I don't want to talk about it because Sally's *dead*. I've been self-sequestered in my little cabin above Truckee for over a month, trying to get over it. She was something special. She'd become my best friend. I tried to save her, I really did. Last I saw her was down in San Pablo Bay, near Roe Island. Then she was gone. That Sally Sturgeon was something special to me."

So Sally never made it up Trout Creek to his cabin! She may not have even gotten through the tunnel under the mountains. Last *I'd* seen her was at Lake Shasta, when Marty the Artist and I dropped her off. Dang it, just when things were looking brighter, I get this news: no Sally.

"But Mr. Carpenter," Doc continued, "the Artist guy who gave me this pontoon boat said he'd *found* your sturgeon friend and taken her to Lake Shasta. Mr. Carpenter, I think she is alive, or at least she was a few weeks ago. The Artist guy talked of this very fish attempting to make a long and dangerous journey to a brook near your cabin. To find you. You knew nothing about this?"

Carpenter sat motionless, gazing across The Lake. Doc folded his arms in his lap and looked away. I tried to be still too; I pulled tight on the ropes tied to the dock.

A tear trickled down Carpenter's right cheek. Doc started to say something, but stopped. The red and white TESSIE flag hung flat vertical against my mast. The left corner of Carpenter's mouth quivered. The mountains that rimmed The Lake glowed pine and fir tree green, but their branches stopped swaying, for an instant, in the Sierra breeze. All the moving waters that drained into The Lake paused. Carpenter's lips parted. His arms rose from his side. Doc looked toward him. The ridges of lake wavelettes held still above their trough companions. Carpenter rose from his seat, head tilted back, and his right arm fired the Sierra Nevada Pale Ale brown bottle toward the pure blue, cloudless sky. While his *"YES!!"* echoed from the Sierra, the wavelete peaks merged with their neighboring troughs, the mountain moving waters cascaded downward, the trees returned to their habit of gentle swaying, and I vibrated from the *kawhomph* of his feet smacking my deck from their brief journey airward.

Sturgeon are perhaps best known for their habit of occasionally jumping completely out of the water for unknown reasons. Colonial records report several incidents of giant sturgeon landing in ships.—Chesapeake Bay Journal, July 1996.

The University had arranged to close off the area surrounding the Highway 89 bridge (Fanny Bridge, the locals call it) and Von Schmidt's famous dam (The Outlet Gates—California Historical Landmark No. 797, the State calls it), where the Truckee River waters leave their Lake cousins and begin the journey over to Nevada. I was tied to the lakeside of the Gates where I watched the birth of the Truckee six feet below. It's always interesting to see a moving water created. One second a water's a lake and the next he or she's a river.

Doc assured Carpenter that it is a fish's natural predeliction to run upstream, and that the only "upstream" available to a fish of Sally's girth was the Truckee River, for, as it was late fall, all the brooks, rivulets and runnels like Trout Creek had dried down to a trickle in preparation for the acceptance of fall rains and winter snows. If she'd made it to Pyramid, she'd be in the Truckee aiming for the Outlet Gates right now. To boost his piscine and moving water credibilities, Doc gave a fifty minute summary of limnology. I listened in—turns out that it's a facinating field of study, indeed. As soon as class was over, Carpenter headed down the Truckee on foot.

Doc's students had fastened a heavy hemp net across the top of the Gates. They weren't sure Sally could do it. They certainly didn't want her crashing onto the top of the Gates or bouncing down the Gate's dam outside face.

When Carpenter came back into sight, hopping upstream from boulder to boulder, waving the famous funnel-hose-duct tape fish listening device over his head, I knew Sally had made it to the Truckee.

Within a half hour they reached the deep pool at the base of the Gates. After a few final words between them, Carpenter climbed the bank, shinnied across the dam, and hopped aboard me. Doc had the students double-check the netting. Carpenter held the aluminum pipe mast with the red and white TESSIE flag in his hands. The dam team was ready. Receiving a thumbs-up from Doc, Carpenter waved the flag above his head, signalling Sally to make her run.

She didn't move. In all the excitement, Carpenter had forgotten that sturgeon can't see worth a damn. Smell good? You bet. And feel and hear pretty well too. Realizing his mistake, he grabbed the sturgeon listening device from my deck and motioned Doc across the Gates toward us. Glancing around to be sure no other *sapien* was within earshot, he said two words to Doc. I've heard them before. I can't repeat them here. They are special words. Doc practiced a few times and when Carpenter was satisfied that Doc had gotten it right, he sent him back across top of the Gates and down the bank to the river.

Doc laid the funnel on the top of the churning waters and placed the hose end in his mouth, cleverly running the device backwards. He trumpeted a signal to Sally below. Nothing happened.

Doc repeated the exercise. Nothing again. Maybe he'd missed the exact pronunciation. Maybe Sally was wary of an unfamiliar voice. Maybe the backwards use of the listening device as a telling device had some subtle technical flaw.

One of the students yelled: "Come on Sally, you can do it!" Soon, the rest of the students and scientists had joined in a chant of "Sally, Sally, Sally." I would have yelled along with them, but, as you know, my inanimacy does not allow it.

"Sally, Sally, Sally."

"Sally, Sally, Sally."

Her head appeared from the bubbling waters.

"Sally, Sally, Sally."

Her tail slapped spray to both banks.

"Sally, Sally, Sally."

Her body arched skyward, proboscis wide open, barbels flopping in the air, half her body in air, half in water. Half a sturgeon dance.

"Sally, Sally, Sally."

"Sally, Sally, Sally."

She submerged. She began swimming in a wide circle, slowly at first; then more rapidly, the arc decreasing, the circle tightening, her speed increasing, and . . .

. . . Sally was on her tail, clear out of the water, sturgeon dancing so pretty that it would've brought tears to the eyes of her great grand-daddy Winslow, made her famous fish-tale telling grand-daddy Ossian lie another great one, and brought pure joy to the hearts of her daughters and sons and grandkids.

And with a final world-class sturgeon surge, she was airborne, aimed right toward me and

Carpenter. The crowd grew silent as the final few feet of her incredible five hundred of mile journey clicked off. And with a great *kersplash* that soaked my deck, roars of "Yeah Sally," and "Way to go Queen of the Sturgeon," and "Hooray, Hooray, Hooray" vibrated the Sierra Nevada air.

It was something. Wish you would have been there to see it.

That night, while the *Acipenser transmontanus* Queen slurped through a heap of the fattest *Pacifastacus leniusculus* that Doc could find, the *sapien* scientists and students (plus a herd of *sapien* Vice Chancellors that Doc had summoned up from the University) celebrated Sally's arrival and planned the next day by sucking down cases of Sierra Nevada Pale Ale. On my deck sat Carpenter, silently sucking with the best of them, listening to the USO project take shape.

The plan was elegant in its simplicity: (1) Use the three current members of the University fleet to haul all the *sapiens* over to Emerald Bay and (2) use the fourth and newest member of the University fleet—Sally herself—to locate and identify Tessie, the Tahoe Monster.

Next afternoon (the USO planning and sipping had gone long into the night), the Yamaha and I, with Carpenter aboard and Sally alongside, joined the flotilla. The Professor stood in the prow of the lead boat, one hand on the brim of his amateur admiral's cap, the other holding the red and white TESSIE pendant, visions of Nobel Laureate no doubt dancing in his head. And with a wave of the flag the U's fleet of four was off, aimed straight across the Lake toward Emerald Bay.

I was the last to arrive. Sally beat me by an hour. It was dusk and I anchored near the others. All the *sapiens* were soon asleep, including Carpenter (University rules prohibited beer drinking when official research was about to be conducted).

Near dawn all the *sapiens,* including Carpenter, were up and at 'em, bright eyed and bushy tailed (a sapien saying Sally found amusing), and I was soon cruising the Emerald Bay waters flanked by my two boat peers, pinging sonar waves across the bottom like crazy. Back and forth, back and forth we went. All day long.

Every once in a while before a back or after a forth, the sonar scope would see something unusual, and Sally would be sent down to take a closer look. Back on top, she'd tell Carpenter through the funnel and hose device what she'd seen. Mostly sunken skiffs and spires of bottom-poking granite. Sometimes lawn chairs or Coleman ice chests.

By the end of the second day, the forths and backs had gotten to me. The place was easy on the eyes, for sure—but how many times can you look at the old gal's Viking Castle before you've memorized every turn of the turrets and stone in the flying buttresses. Or wonder about the solitary life of old Hermit Barter who lived on the little island that protruded from the middle of the bay.

The students seemed to enjoy themselves. They collected water samples for future planketon counts back at the lab, went for noontime dips, and constantly took The Lake's temperature. The Lake's temperature hardly varies more than a degree. Hard to imagine getting excited over a change in a Celsius decimal point. Maybe I don't appreciate the true rewards of a career in The Sciences.

By the end of the third day, Carpenter was so unhappy that he threatened Doc with the imminent withdrawal of his part of the team, including the deep-diving, sonar-verifying, talking sturgeon. Before nightfall, a case of the Official brew was icing in the former fish tank in my left pontoon. That seemed to help.

On the fourth afternoon, a great fall storm swept across The Lake. Even the coziness of Emerald Bay offered no protection. Carpenter went to shore for the night, retreating with the rest of the *sapiens* to the cold but dry *Vikingsholm*. I was left anchored in shallow water just off shore. Sally slept on the sandy bottom just below me. By midnight, ten foot waves white-capped by the wind were heaving me up and down and spinning me about. Dang it all, was I ever lakesick. The fury finally broke loose my anchor and I was swept across the bay toward the tiny Emerald Isle. Ooh, I was so scared. We never had storms like this back on The River. Snow soon piled up on me, railing deep. The fish tank lid on my left pontoon blew off, the remaining beers floated out, and the tank filled with lake water. Oooh, I was listing so bad. Icicles hung from the Yamaha. The cute TESSIE flag had long since disappeared. My single pontoon buoyancy was no match for the weight of water, snow and ice. The rocky shore of the Isle of Emerald loomed not twenty yards away. Uoooh, I was a goner for sure if I wacked the granite sides of it. My pontoons would crumple up like a wad of tin foil. My new plywood deck would be smashed to smithereens. And poor Yamaha—just an innocent bystander—would be fifty fathoms deep if we smacked that island. Ten yards and heading right for it.

Hey, it looks further. Hey, what's up? I'm moving backwards and I'm rising. Whoa there.

What's this? There's a giant something under me. Holy carp, I'm on the back of a big fish.
I mean, this is a *big* fish. Neptune alive, would 'ya look at those diamond shaped scutes.

When the clear dawn broke over Emerald Bay, the *sapiens* were up and on the beach. One
of the big boats was gone, presumably sunk. The other could be seen adrift, far out in
The Lake. I was beached and bruised, but alive. Well, not alive exactly, but certainly not
disassembled.

Carpenter waded into the bay and Sally rose to greet him.

"You okay, Sally Sturgeon?" he asked.

"I'm just fine, Carpenter. Really fine. Really, really fine," she smiled.

"What's to be so happy about? This place is a hell of a mess. There's junk and debris
everywhere, a boat's sunk, and old Pontoon looks like he's been through a destruction
derby."

"Found my pop."

"Excuse me, what'd you say Sally?"

"Found my pop."

"You found your pop. I must be translating wrong. What does that mean?"

"My pop. My father."

"Oh Sally, all that tossing and turning under water last night has you dizzy and confused.
You know your dad disappeared before you were born. You've told me so, many a time."

"Found him."

"You found him. Where?"

"Here. He saved Pontoon from crashing on the rocks of that island out there," Sally said,
tilting her snout sideways.

"Your pop is here in Lake Tahoe?"

"Yep, is he ever. All two thousand pounds of him. He's a big one, that's for sure. Big, but
sweet. Want to meet him?"

"Can he talk and hear me?" asked Carpenter.

"Don't think so. But I can translate. Hop on the pontoon boat and cruise out a ways.
Pop's too big to come in this close to shore."

"Can I bring the Professor along?"

"Sure. See you in a few minutes."

After Carpenter and Doc bilged out my left pontoon and fed the Yamaha some fresh gasoline and oil, we putt-putted toward the middle of Emerald Bay. Sally rose after we'd coasted to a stop. Doc waved to her nervously. Carpenter yelled a "we're here!" and placed the sturgeon hearing aide on the top of the water.

"Pop, want you to meet my best *sapien* friend, name is Carpenter. He's from the Sacramento River down in the valley. Calls it The River. Oh, and this pontoon boat is an old friend too. Up on the deck there is a guy they call Doc. He's a limnologist. He's been looking for you for years, especially the last week. I think it would make all of them happy if you could rise up and show them your stuff."

With that, the old sturgeon filled his air bladder and floated to the surface on my starboard. He was nearly as long as me and about half as wide.

"Pleased to meet you, sir," said Carpenter. "Any relative of my best friend Sally is a friend of mine. It's quite an honor. Boy, you *are* big."

"Crawdads," yelled Doc. "I knew it. I just knew it. Stick a sturgeon in a pond with a zillion crawdads, and you'd expect something like this. He's our TESSIE, no doubt about it. Oh boy oh boy oh boy, I'm gonna be famous. Wait until the National Science Foundation hears about this; they'll give me millions. Wait until the University's public relations team gets the cameras rolling and gets that big boy on film. I'll get a new office and a merit raise. I'll get my own cable channel. The Sturgeon Station, I'll call it. Can I interview him Sally? Huh, huh? Can I, now? Huh? Can I, can I?"

"What cameras?" asked Carpenter.

"You mean the ones from the University over on shore?" said Doc. "Oh, there's more coming than that, don't you worry. While you were readying the pontoon boat, I made a few calls. There's a helicopter on its way from a Reno television station as we speak. The National Geographic Society will be here by afternoon. And Mike Wallace and the entire Sixty Minutes crew should be here by tomorrow."

Carpenter motioned to Sally and they moved to my stern. He crouched and said something I couldn't catch. She nodded sideways, an unmistakable "no." He shook his fist toward the bow where Doc remained. Another sideways motion. He pointed to her still-surfaced dad, then again to the Professor at the bow, then to the shore where the other scientist-*sapiens* were now standing and a horde of media-*sapiens* soon would, all the while speaking to her firmly though quietly so that neither Doc nor I could hear. This exchange went on for a few minutes, his arms flailing wilder, her head and tail nodding and waving faster, as the discussion became more heated. Finally, he jumped up, yelled "I give up. You drive me crazy, you. . . you. . . stupid sturgeon," and threw the famous funnel and hose listening device past her. With a swish of her considerable tail, she soaked him head to toe in retribution, did a quick half out of the water dance, and disappeared, her behemoth papa following. Carpenter, who clearly had lost the argument, turned to Doc and spoke slowly and carefully.

"You know what Professor? Some things are best left alone. Some people are happier when left to wonder and imagine and pretend. And some things are best not explained by science. You know what Professor? Sally and I agree that this is one of those things. We just don't agree on what to do with you. You're lucky she won the argument; yes sir, lucky you are."

And with that, Carpenter shoved the good doctor overboard. No sooner had the echo of the splash returned from Emerald Isle than a foot and a half diameter proboscis opened beneath the floundering scientist. Oh my goodness, Sally's dad is going to inhale Doc and gizzard-grind him to death! Oh lordy, I'm about to become an accomplice to piscine murder, I thought as the bottom half of Doc disappeared into the great orifice. We'll be on the lamb for sure, me and two sturgeon and a crazy sapien from Sacramento, dodging the FBI. The Coast Guard will track us down and shoot me full of holes, I thought as Doc disappeared.

A roaring *petuewey* broke the surface as Sally's dad launched Doc like a Poseidon missile. Limnological profanity echoed across the water as the temporarily airborne Professor arched toward shore. With a memorable *kerplash* that showered his students and the film crew alike, Doc found himself butt first and chin deep in the shallows of Emerald Bay, ready for his first interview. And his last, for though Sally had spared Doc (contrary to Carpenter's advice, it was now clear), she was not about to let her pop—the great Fish King of Lake Tahoe, the TESSIE of *sapien* dreams—become the object of some *sapien* sideshow.

Carpenter fired up the Yamaha and the four of us were off, Sally to port, her pop to starboard, and the Emerald Isle and Doc to stern. My two still-shiny aluminum pontoons cut a handsome pair of wakes on the glassy morning surface of Lake Tahoe. "Some things are best left imagined," said Carpenter. "Don't you agree, Mr. Pontoon?"

"Couldn't agree more, " I replied.

A BRIEF AUTOBIOGRAPHY

by The Sacramento River

"The Sacramento and San Joaquin rivers empty
into the Bay of San Francisco at the same point,
about sixty miles from the Pacific, and by
numerous mouths, or sloughs as they are called.
These sloughs wind through an immense
timbered swamp, and constitute a terraqueous
labyrinth of such intricacy, that unskillful
and inexperienced navigators have been
lost for many days in it, and some,
I have been told, have perished,
never finding their way out."

Edwin Bryant, *What I Saw in California*, 1848.

When I was younger—before your Shasta-high dams and Orovillian lakes, before the peat levees of the post-gold rush Delta reclamation, before Sutter's settlement compounded down the lettered streets of Sacramento and tumbled to a halt at my bank, before you traipsed my great Valley and sailed vainly for the gate to my Bay—I was free.

Before any of *you* arrived on the lands of California, my sister the San Joaquin and I could stretch nearly its full length. And when a multitude of distant cousins, air-born aqueous far out over the Pacific, would drop by to visit in winter and spring, I could lap the feet of the

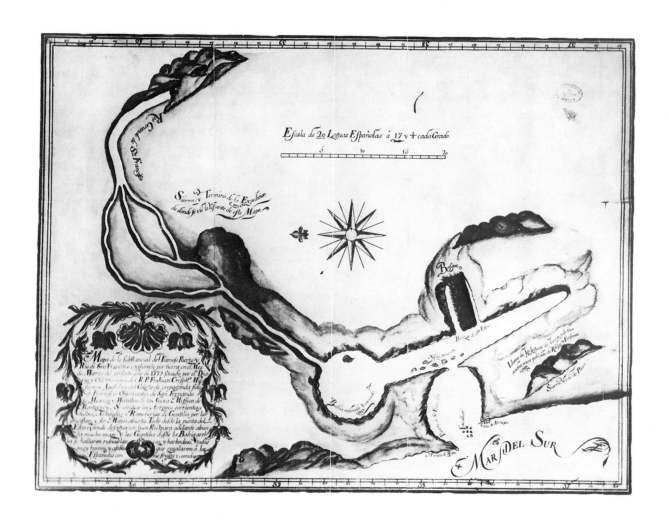

Father Crespi Map: 1772

Coast and Sierra ranges, filling the Great Valley head to toe, one side to the other. It was really something, spreading out like that.

Back then my sister had her own lake, Tulare Lake. Depending on the season, she'd run right through it, or drain into it, maybe seep out of it. I had one too, called Goose Lake. My Pit River arm once got water from it. I used to be able to reach into Oregon through the Pit and Goose. Nowadays, I claim the top of the South Fork of the Pit as my true headwater, though some of you disagree. By the way, that HEADWATERS of the SACRAMENTO RIVER sign by the spring in the City Park of the City of Mt. Shasta *really* bugs me.

You once wished me to start far to the east and run all the way to the Pacific, like some slipped-south Northwest Passage. I've seen the hoped-for me on old maps, entering the kingdom of Calafia labeled variously: Buenaventura, Bonaventura, Rio Grande de San Francisco, Jesus Maria and Rio Sacramento.

You and my names! You once called my upper part the Destruction River. I didn't care much for that. That and the damn levee building.

When the first few went up, down in the Delta where my sister and I meet, I said to her: "Hey, relax. What's a couple of new riverbanks? We can still slough and anabranch here, backwater and oxbow there." Well, had I known, I would've put a stop to it right then and there. Gave you a berm, you took a whole island. Conceded you an island, you raised a new levee. New levee here, new levee there, pretty soon I had to sleep on my side at night, it got so cramped.

And my top and bottom! While I was watching you raise my Delta, you snuck up North and damed me, and snuck down past my sister and drained her, and sluiced around the Sierra foothills washing dirt for gold and filled me with silt. Why, I used to be clear and clean. Now look at me. Aren't you embarrassed?

And my friends piscine. The ones born here, my natives, not those stripped bass and cat-fish foreigners you threw in me. How do you think my salmon feel, running up me each year, no where to spawn?

And don't even get me started on my sturgeon friends.

So it's Destruction you once called me and it's destruction you got. Do you think it's easy being a once-great river? Have any of you ever tried? I don't think there's a one of you out there who could even be a pond or a snowflake, let alone a river. Let alone a trapped one. I mean, what did you expect would happen when you squished-in my sides and silted-up my bottom and re-routed my delta?

Look, I'm still willing to try and work with you. Especially you Delta folks; I like you guys and I know you have problems too, and I know that, sometimes, things have to change. I hear from my relatives all around the world that it isn't just me. Times are tough for *all* the moving waters.

I'll tell you what. Do a couple of things for me and I'll swear to Mother Nature that I'll be nice. Cross my tributaries and hope to evaporate.

First: the dam thing. Forget the dam thing. Bridges? You bet; never met a bridge that I didn't respect. Docks, marinas, house boats? No problemo, as long as they stay afloat. But dams? No thank you. I'm not a happy watercourse when I'm blocked by concrete. So no more dams; OK?

Second: let me stretch once in a while, will ya? You know those winters or springs when Mother Nature gets the instructions to the Pacific storms all mixed up, and she sends *everyone* here at once? (Like she did this past winter, though I hate to bring that up cause I hear you're still pretty upset about last winter.) Well, when The Mother goofs up like that, just open up a few more weirs, concede a little more farmland, maybe give me back a couple more Delta islands. I need a little more elbow room; deal?

I got to tell you: if I had known how it would all turn out when I first saw you guys, when I saw Sergeant Sanchez's scow round the bend at Sherman Island that morning on 23 October 1811 and became the first ever to enter me, well, I would have capsized the little craft and sent he and the padres swimming home. Buenaventura, indeed.

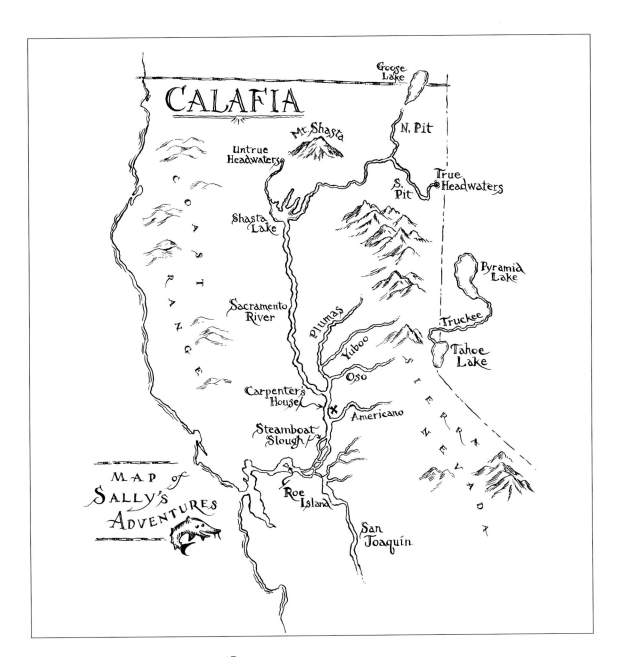

COLOR REPRODUCTIONS

MT. DIABLO AND THE DELTA, 23 X 45 In., Watercolor, 1995, cover,
Courtesy of: Charlie and Janie Soderquist

WINTER MIST, 40 X 36 In., Oil on canvas, 1995, page 4,
Courtesy of: Adrienne Young

SUMMER EVENING IN THE MEADOWS, 16 X 33 In., Watercolor, 1995, page 5,
Courtesy of: Christopher Jensen

REFLECTING SKY, 84 X 72 In., Oil on canvas, 1994, page 8,
Courtesy of: Marty Stanley

SUMMER ON THE SACRAMENTO, 24 X 58 In., Watercolor, 1991, page 9,
Courtesy of: Raley's Corporate Collection

THE SAN JOAQUIN, 22 X 49 In., Watercolor, 1991, page 10,
Courtesy of: The Kaiser Permanente Collection, Stockton, California

ELK SLOUGH, 27 X 50 In., Watercolor, 1993, page 12,
Courtesy of: Marji and Phil Dunn

SPRING ON SUTTER SLOUGH, 28 X 56 In., Watercolor, 1992, page 14,
Courtesy of: The Marguerite Barsoom Estate

WATER HYACINTH, 28 X 36 In., Watercolor, 1992, page 21,
Courtesy of: Mary and Chris Fulster

MEADOWS SUNSET, 18 X 40 In., Watercolor, 1992, page 42,
Courtesy of: George Myers

SHADOWS ACROSS THE SLOUGH, 30 X 36 In., Watercolor, 1991, page 48,
Courtesy of: Joan and Ted Phillips

SUMMER EVENING SKY, 34 X 60 In., Oil on canvas, 1994, page 60,
Courtesy of: Brian Machado

MORNING LIGHT ON ELK SLOUGH, 30 X 32 In., Oil on canvas, 1994, page 64,
Courtesy of: The Wilke, Fleury, Hoffelt, Gould & Birney Collection

EVENING COLORS, 18 X 41 In., Watercolor, 1992, page 84,
Courtesy of: Chiles Wilson

WINTER ON STEAMBOAT SLOUGH, 32 X 45 In., Watercolor, 1990, page 86,
Courtesy of: Sandy and Darrell Ferreira

BACON ISLAND, 22 X 48 In., Watercolor, 1991, page 112,
Courtesy of: The Kaiser Permanente Collection, Stockton, California

MISTY RIVER EVENING, 16 X 39 In., Watercolor, 1991, page 114,
Courtesy of: The Kleinfelder Inc. Collection

RIVER MIST, 22 X 52 In., Watercolor, 1992, page 142,
Courtesy of: The Kaiser Permanente Collection, Stockton, California

PHOTO CREDITS

Pages 7, 71, 83: Courtesy of The Portland Museum
Page 63: from *Maps of California*, Cadwalader Ringgold, 1851

SLOUGH * MAIN CANAL * NORTH CANAL * NORTH
MOKELUMNE RIVER * ROARING RIVER SLOUGH
NORTH VICTORIA CANAL * NOYCE SLOUGH * HAA
SLOUGH * TOM PAINE SLOUGH * MAYBERRY CUT
TAYLOR SLOUGH * MANDEVILLE CUT * DENVERTO
SLOUGH * BOYNTON SLOUGH * CORDELIA SLOUGH
MARSHALL CUT * SAND MOUND SLOUGH * SUTTE
SLOUGH * BISHOP CUT * PARADISE CUT * LITTL
POTATO SLOUGH * SMITH CANAL * BROAD SLOUG
* CALAVERAS RIVER * VOLANTI SLOUGH * BURN
CUTOFF * GOODYEAR SLOUGH * CONNECT SLOUG
* LITTLE CONNECTION SLOUGH * TURNER CUT
NURSE SLOUGH * WHITE SLOUGH * FROST SLOUG
* PIPER SLOUGH * HEADREACH CUTOFF * MIDDL
RIVER * CROSS SLOUGH * LUCO SLOUGH * WAR
CUT * FALSE RIVER * SACRAMENTO RIVER * HO
SLOUGH * WOODWARD CANAL * LATHAM SLOUGH
FRANK HORAN SLOUGH * TURNER CUT * PEYTONI
SLOUGH * GALLAGHER SLOUGH * SHELDRAKE SLOUG
* FABIAN AND BELL CANAL * THE MEADOWS SLOUG
SYCAMORE SLOUGH * GEORGIANA SLOUGH * WELL